A WIZARDS OF LITTLE HOPE COZY MYSTERY

WIZARDLY WOES

TYLER RHODES

Preface

Please note, this series takes place in the United Kingdom. I have purposefully used British spelling. You'll hardly notice a difference, but color is colour, gray is grey, center is centre, and a few other minor differences.

This cozy mystery is set in the beautiful heart of England where one wizard and his family seem to get into more bother than is either fair or sensible.

You can expect no bad language, a hefty dose of snappy banter, and a love interest that isn't too slow burn because our main characters are in their thirties, and who has the time to mess around? We also, of course, have plenty of murders to be solved. Expect mystery, red herrings, and a large cast of magical miscreants. Each book will give you an oversized slice of paranormal action. All ending with a satisfying conclusion.

As with all, hopefully, good fiction, my characters are based firmly in reality, and then we get to go off on a mad one!

Enjoy a comforting, rollicking good yarn, as a group of best friends, who just happen to be related wizards, band together to solve mysteries and murders. It's about time the guys got some "cozy" action, don't you think?

With an array of characters including Grenadine the super-sentient spider, a grumpy hedgehog, an Irish Wolfhound familiar named Kale, and the extended family, I hope you immerse yourself in this first in series. Plenty more to come.

Oh, and don't forget the gnomes.

Tyler

I send out emails when new books are published, so please sign up for news about releases and sales. No spam. Just book updates. Promise.

Bran's Dream

"Burty Fizzingbuns, you put that back. Bellpepper, it's too heavy for you, honey, let Betty do it. Bignoodle, help Betty. Posy Nibbler, Dipple Sprocket, and Bingles, I've told you all a thousand times, that's where the crystals are meant to be. Stop mixing up the colours. It just gets confusing." I smiled despite the mayhem. I wouldn't have it any other way.

Maybe I'd have a few less "helpers" if I had the choice, but at least the price is appropriate. Free, if I provide lodging and food. And it means I always have company when at work, which is both a blessing and a curse. Sometimes I like boring, quiet, slow times, but there's always one drama or another.

Speaking of which.

Standin'—and yes, his surname is Yergarden— knocked his hat off when he tried to align a dreamcatcher, glared at the offending article constructed over several days from feathers of the generous birds I have an arrangement with, then cursed like only he can, thankfully in a language I don't understand, and scowled at the others as they giggled merrily.

I sighed—the hundredth of the day, and it was only half past nine—as I padded over and helped arrange the display. Gawn Fishin' had a hook stuck in a scarf, so I helped him with that and warned him about practising casting in the shop. Again.

The bell above the door jangled so I told everyone, "Look sharp," then retreated into the cubbyhole where I spend a great deal of my time because the shop is so crowded with shelves, racks, displays, and what have you that I take up too much floor space.

"Welcome to Bran's Dream," I said, smiling at the tourist couple as they stood just inside the door, taking in the various offerings that greeted them like a slap in the face with a limp wand dipped in patchouli.

The man grunted, ignoring me completely, the kindly-looking woman smiled and asked, "Do you have dreamcatchers? I promised my grandson one."

"Of course, right over there." I pointed at the neat display and watched as they wandered over.

They studied the various trinkets as they shuffled through the cramped aisles, picking up crystals, frowning at horrendous scarves, and bewildered by the numerous pipes and other ways to ingest medicinal herbs.

"Look how dirty it is in here," complained the man with a scowl.

"It's spotless. Not a speck of dust. See?" The woman ran her hand across a shelf and showed her husband her clean finger.

"What about that? It's a massive cobweb. And look at that spider. It's huge." He took a step back and pointed.

"Aw, isn't it cute?" She turned to me and asked, "Is it part of the shop? Are the spider and web real?"

"It's real. That's Grenadine. She hates having her web disturbed, and she's been here longer than I have," I said, smiling.

"How delightful!" she clapped as she got close to Grenadine and studied her.

"Did that wrinkly old man call me fat?" asked Grenadine.

"No, he said you were big. There's a difference."

"Good, because otherwise I'd bite him."

"You better not," I warned. "He looks like he might bite you back."

"Sorry, what was that?" asked the lady.

"Nothing, just talking to the spider," I said happily, knowing that tourists love this kind of stuff. After all, it's why they come. The chance to experience real magic, even though most believe it's just a gimmick.

"Marvellous. Is it your familiar?"

"No, just a chatty spider."

"What a load of nonsense. Stupid hippies. As if spiders can talk," grumbled the man as he scowled at Grenadine and the world in general. This was not somebody who appreciated the magic life had to offer.

"Oh, look at the cute gnomes," squealed the nice lady.

"We are not getting gnomes," snapped her husband.

"Not even a small one? What about him with the massive nose?" She called out, "What's his name?"

"That's Bignoodle. But they aren't for sale. See the sign?"

Like so many customers before her, she turned back to the table and read the sign out loud above the now stationary gnomes. "Not for sale. Please do not touch. They don't like it." She looked my way and joked, "Will they kick me if I pick one up?"

"They might," I warned, laughing along when in truth it was a distinct possibility.

"Can you just choose a feathery thing and let me get out of here? This incense is playing havoc with my allergies," whined the grump.

"Go wait outside, then. I'll only be a minute."

He didn't need telling twice. He stomped out of the shop with his clean walking boots, tanned legs going as fast as he was able.

Kale wandered over and sniffed the lady's hand, making her jump.

"Oh my, you're a big fellow, aren't you?"

"Does she want me to answer?" Kale asked me, his words nothing but a series of staccato barks for anyone not in tune with my ever-present companion.

I shook my head at him then told the lady, "This is Kale. He likes people and is a big softy, but sorry he made you jump."

"An Irish Wolfhound! I love the breed. They're so gentle and kind." She bent, and she didn't have to bend much, and met Kale's kind brown eyes. "Hello. Would you like a treat?"

Kale barked a yes and she pulled out a dog biscuit from her lightweight jacket pocket. He took it gently then swallowed it in one go. A long line of drool hung from his mouth.

"You always have biscuits in your pocket?" I called over, tone light.

"Yes, don't you?"

"Er, yeah, I do," I admitted.

Grenadine dropped down on a single thread and landed between Kale's ears. He moved to shake her off, then obviously remembered what happened last time, so merely sighed. The super-sentient spider—her personal description —pointed with two legs, as if directing operations, and Kale ignored her completely, hoping she would leave faster.

Kale padded into the cubby, groaned, then curled up under the bench behind me and closed his eyes. He likes two things in life. Eating and sleeping. Grenadine settled too, curling her legs in and murmuring sweetly about how soft her hairy bed was.

Several minutes later, the sweet lady came over with a selection of dreamcatchers, a scarf, a pack of incense, stickers with the shop logo on, and a bong. I raised an eyebrow and she tittered as she said, "Helps with the arthritis."

"That's what a lot of customers say. Anything else?"

She leaned forward, checked there were no other customers, then whispered, "Are you the guy that can murder my husband if the price is right?"

I shifted until our noses almost touched, then told her, "I even sell body bags in tie-dye. They're over by the scarves. You must have missed them." Her eyes twinkled with mirth, and she even turned to look, then laughed as I said, "Gotcha!"

"You're funny," she tittered, hand over her mouth.

"So are you. You had me for a minute there."

"I did, didn't I?" she said, still smiling. "What do I owe you?" She looked past me and did a double-take like lots of others. "Is that a hedgehog? Gosh, this is a busy place. You must love animals."

"I do. And it is. She likes to stay warm. She has her own comfy bed on that bench and mostly sleeps. Don't tell anyone," I said, leaning close again, "but it's actually my mother. She's a witch, or was, and she shifted into hedgehog form one evening and got stuck. Now she lives here, but there's a hedgehog flap in the back door so she can come and go as she pleases. Poor thing's a bit grumpy, but that's understandable."

"My, I'm so glad I came. You are such a joker. I'll be sure to tell our friends."

"A happy customer is a returning customer," I said, leaving out the bit about not joking. Mum's been stuck this way for three years and had shown no sign of returning to human form any time soon. At least she drinks less this way, although sometimes I wonder as some mornings the shop stinks of local beer when I come to open up.

She settled up and I wrapped her purchases carefully.

"Thank you. Um, what's your name?"

"I'm Branok. Everyone calls me Bran."

"Ah, I get the name of the shop now. Bran's Dream. But why dream?"

"Two reasons. When I bought the shop three years ago and finally had my own business, it was like a dream come true. No more working for 'The Man' for me. Being my own boss has been great. But I guess the main reason is because sometimes, quite often actually, life feels like a dream. Don't you think?" It was a conversation I've had countless times with customers, but it's always interesting to see what their answer will be.

"Absolutely! And when you get to my age and look back on your life, it does feel like it could have been a dream. Currently," she confided, "I'm in a nightmare, though. My husband is not a fan of what he calls 'hippy nonsense,' but he just doesn't understand. This is a magical place. I can feel it."

"Sure is. I bet he isn't that bad really."

"His heart's in the right place, but he's old-fashioned. I wanted to get a reading. Maybe you can do the Tarot tomorrow? I can send him off walking for a few hours."

"It would be my pleasure. And you are?"

"Sheila. Everyone calls me Sheila," she joked. "That grumpy old man, Albert, and I are having a little tour of the country before we're too ancient. Spent a fortune on a compact campervan. Let's just say it's been a long six weeks and I'm looking forward to going home. This heatwave hasn't helped. We need rain."

"Sure do," I agreed. It's been the main topic of conversation for a month now. Nobody is used to the heat, and rain is usually as common as a fish and chips supper in these parts. "Oh, there's always the cliff," I said, miming pushing someone off. "Up at the old quarry above the woods. Nice and high."

"Don't put ideas in my head," she chuckled. With a nod, she gathered her purchases, put them into her bag for life, then weaved her way to the door. "See you tomorrow. Do I need an appointment?"

"How about twelve? I close then, so we won't be disturbed."

"Perfect. Bye then. Oh, and bye, Kale. What a funny name for a dog." She was gone with a tinkle of the bell.

Kale snored, oblivious. Grenadine opened several eyes then fell back to sleep.

"Okay fellas, coast's clear," I told the gnomes.

The bickering began immediately. Just another day in the shop like so many others. I love it. Familiar, safe, warm. A steady routine that keeps me from the darkness that threatens to send me spiralling down into depression if I let it. But I won't, and haven't for years.

Life is good. My wife may be gone, a death I will never truly recover from, but I've got my act together, am doing well, and have finally found peace and meaning since coming home. After a long time, I feel like I belong somewhere again. Somewhere, and to people. Animals too. Oh, and the gnomes and plenty of others. But it is Kale I have to give the most credit to. When he appeared outside the shop the day I came to view it, I knew we would be the best of friends. We haven't spent a day apart since. I think, more than anything, it was him that convinced me to buy the place and realise I'd made the right decision coming home.

He was just a pup then, but already huge. This is how it happens in Little Hope. Your familiar finds you, or you find them, and you just click. A large piece of the whole you didn't know was missing until the connection is made.

The rest of the morning was busy, but business trailed off close to lunchtime as tourists began to heed the call of their growling stomachs and turned their attention to investigating the various cafes and restaurants of Little Hope. I entered the cubby and turned on the old, small TV fixed high to the wall, and settled back to catch the local news.

The sprightly news reporter beamed, then became serious as she read a news report that left me cold yet sweating. When it was over, I clicked off the TV with the remote and just sat there stunned.

"Wasn't that the name of the grumpy man who was in here earlier with his wife?" asked Kale, nudging my leg with his nose.

"It was," I groaned, my head spinning.

"And didn't you tell her to push him off the cliff at the old quarry above the woods?"

"I might have jokingly suggested it, yes." I sighed, rubbing at my temples like it might make all this go away.

"And didn't that reporter say that the man, Albert, apparently fell from that very cliff?"

"She did."

"That's quite a coincidence."

"I know it is! What am I supposed to do now?"

"Should you report it?" asked Kale, nuzzling in tight so I'd rub his head.

"Yes. No. Maybe. I don't know. Calum will not be happy to see me, and it's probably just a coincidence. Yes, it has to be." I chuckled to myself, shaking my head. "Sheila was a sweet lady. She isn't going to just go and murder her husband right after us joking about shoving him off that very cliff. Right?" I turned to Kale, hoping he'd help.

"She did seem nice. But what if she isn't? What if they had an argument while on a walk and then she remembered what you said and just did it without thinking? These things happen."

"Do they? I know we get the occasional accident as there are a lot of hikers around, but deaths are very rare. And as for murder. Ugh, what a mess."

"Bran, just call the Police Chief. I know you and Calum don't get along, but this is important. You don't have to meet face-to-face, just call."

I brightened at the idea. "You're right! I can just call. I wish he could put what happened behind him, but he won't. Or can't. But yes, this is important. Or, probably not. It was an accident. It has to be. I'll phone and tell him, just so he knows, but I'm sure it was a terrible accident. Poor Sheila. She must be distraught. What a horrible thing to happen."

Before I could second-guess myself, I picked up the handset and called a number I hadn't used in a very long time.

"What do you want, Bran?" came the weary voice of Police Chief Calum Swift. My ex father-in-law, and as far as he was concerned, I was the man who killed his daughter, my beautiful wife.

"I have information about the death of that man up at the quarry," I blurted, my stomach in knots.

"You didn't waste much time," he snapped. "I don't want you or your family interfering. I can deal with this accident without you offering any of your special kind of help."

My heart skipped a beat as I asked, "It was an accident?"

"Of course! Why are you calling me? I have nothing to say to you." The line crackled and I missed what he said next.

"Calum, can you hear me?"

"Yes. Leave me alone, Bran."

"I need to tell you something. He was in the shop earlier with his wife. I was chatting with Sheila. Joking around. She was saying about her husband being a grump and I jokingly said maybe she could push him off the cliff." The line crackled again and I said, "Hello? Can you hear me?"

"Yes, I can hear you. Don't call me again. The death was an accident. His wife wasn't with him, not that it's any of your business. I do not want to hear your voice ever again. Understand? These damn local reporters. Albert's name shouldn't even have been mentioned. It's not how things are done." Calum hung up.

"He'll come around eventually," said Kale as he rested his chin on my lap.

"I don't think he'll ever forgive me for us losing Emily. He thought the world of her. So did I."

"I know you did. What's the verdict? What did Calum say?"

"That it was an accident and he hates me. The line was a bit crackly, but he said Sheila wasn't with Albert so I guess that's that."

"So why so glum?"

"It just doesn't feel right. I'm not sure he heard me properly, or didn't want to. But if Sheila wasn't there I suppose it doesn't matter."

"Then you did the right thing. That's good news, Bran. Okay, maybe not good news, but at least now we know that poor woman didn't do anything untoward."

"I guess."

So why didn't this feel right? Was it because of my history with Calum that I had this knot in my stomach? Or was it something else?

Chance Encounters

At lunchtime I shut up shop for the usual hour. Normally, I'll go hang with Forest and Roger, but they were on a rush job today and said they would eat on the go. That was fine. It meant I could have my favourite for lunch and just relax. Try to put the conversation with Calum, and the thought of poor Sheila, out of my mind. Despite the pain in my belly, I salivated at the thought of what awaited.

"Kale, you fancy getting some lunch?" Like I had to ask.

"Did I meet the Devil and teach him a thing or two?" he asked, dodging expertly between the stock and exiting the shop while I held the door open.

Grenadine scuttled along Kale's nose, under his chin, then down his back before leaping off his tail and dashing to her lair. She still hasn't built up the courage to leave the shop yet.

"Was that rhetorical?"

"Did it sound rhetorical?"

I frowned as I studied my best friend, although I never told my housemates that. "Yes, that's why I asked. But now I'm wondering if you asking if it was rhetorical was rhetorical too."

"Let's just go get lunch," sighed Kale, drooling as he sat patiently waiting for me to lock up.

"What you going to get?" I asked him.

We both laughed at the old joke. We knew exactly what we were going to eat.

The heat hit with a surprise, same as it has every day for week upon week. The West Midlands is usually wet and relatively cool even in the height of summer, but this year, and for several before it, we've had heatwaves that leave our pretty market town's two thousand or so residents gasping. It doesn't stop the tourists coming, though. In fact, the hotter it gets, the more they seem to pour in to our cobbled streets and the various campsites and holiday homes dotted around the area.

Normally a stickler for Levi's and boots along with a faded t-shirt and a leather jacket in the cooler months, I've been living in cut-offs, vests, and flip-flops for what seems like forever. Even my curly brown hair is beginning to get on my nerves and I'm contemplating getting the lot shaved off, but can't face the hairdressers. Just the thought of sitting in the chair and having to make small talk while a madman assaults me with sharp instruments makes me shudder. And our local hairdresser is not someone you get to tell how you'd like your hair. I'll continue to suffer, just not in silence.

Kale and I shuffled up Wizard's Way, the main high street that runs from the top of town down to the bottom where I have my shop. The road was cobbled over in the nineties, a unanimous decision of the residents and Town Council, and ever since then, and with the other more "quaint" modifications to our town, Little Hope has thrived.

We've always been a mecca for the different, but for many years it was mostly locals who knew our town wasn't like any other. Slowly, everyone began to capitalise on our uniqueness. More esoteric shops opened, more magic was performed, more supernaturals came and decided to stay, and over generations our town has become what some see as a dumping ground for dispossessed supernaturals and oddballs, but what the locals see as a badge of honour. A home for those that won't conform, don't want to conform, and can't even if they try.

I'd tried, but here I am, back where I truly belong.

Kale and I smiled and said our hellos as we made our way up the hill, passing tourists dressed in everything from high-end walking gear to head-to-toe tie-dye. Others rode their bikes, enjoying the luxury of being able to cycle around a town devoid of cars. Businesses have an hour before and after shop hours to load and unload goods, but otherwise it's as if you've stepped back in time.

Kale lifted his leg and peed halfway up a vintage lamp post, sighed happily, then muttered about people letting their dogs pee in his territory. I kept my mouth shut; I knew better than to argue with a guy and his territorial nature.

The closer we got to our destination, the faster Kale and I walked.

"You hungry?" I chuckled. "I can hear your stomach growling."

"Starving. Oh boy, I can't wait."

"Me neither." My own stomach rumbled in anticipation and we followed the unmistakable aroma of freshly baked goods, the scent drifting on a gentle, but very welcome breeze as it made its way sluggishly down Wizard's Way.

"Ah, Lovely Buns," I sighed.

"Excuse me?" snapped a woman as she stopped dead in her tracks, frowning as she put her hands indignantly on her hips.

"Lovely Buns," I said, smiling.

"How dare you?" she growled, but then her eyes softened and her posture changed as she took me and Kale in. "Oh, what a lovely dog. Is he a Great Dane?"

"No, he's an Irish Wolfhound."

"Look at his lovely fur. So brown and long like a big old cuddly teddy bear." She reached out to stroke Kale, but he took a step back.

"You should always ask first," I told her.

"Oh, gosh, sorry. How rude. Although, you were rather rude too." She smiled, and cocked her head to the side, brushing pale blond locks away from a nicely tanned face. Her blue eyes almost made me sink to my knees and thank the big wizard in the sky for such wonders.

Dimples made her cheeks good enough to eat. Not that I'm in the habit of eating the cheeks of strangers. Or people I know. Her cut-off faded denim shorts rode high, revealing bronzed thighs.

I got a delicious smell of apple blossom as she played with her hair, making me picture bright spring days and the joy of mowing the lawn, watching the bees buzz about the garden.

"I was?" I asked, distracted by the mental imagery and her glorious aroma. "How was I rude?"

"About the lovely buns. Normally, I'd slap a guy for something like that."

I laughed as I pointed to the sign above the shop we were standing outside. She reddened and blurted, "Oh, gosh, I am so sorry. I'm such an idiot. Ugh, I can't seem to do a thing right since I got back. Everything's so different. It's all so much more..."

"Intense?" I asked, smiling as she squirmed.

"Yes, that's it. Intense. I don't remember it being quite so..."

"Mad as a box of frogs?"

"Exactly. I'm Helen by the way. Helen Granger. And you are?"

"I'm Branok. Everyone calls me Bran. Bran Fairfield."

"You're Bran? No way. You should be what, mid-thirties now? Same as me. Look at you." She gave me the once over, clearly not too disappointed. Good job she hadn't seen me five years ago. I was more like a ball wearing boots and a baseball cap held together by nothing more than hope.

"And look at you. Little Helen Granger. We used to play together. Do you remember?"

"I do. Wow, we hung out all the time. We were right terrors, weren't we? Always getting into mischief. My parents used to have a fit over the state I came home in."

Helen's spirit darkened at the mention of her parents. It had been a sad time for her and the whole town when it happened.

"I'm so sorry about your dad. It didn't really mean much back then when we were so young. But it must have been tough for you and your mum. You moved away. Sorry, that was lame. You already know that."

Helens's sparkle returned and she laughed at my nonsense. "Mum needed a fresh start, and she was never into the alternative stuff like Dad was. We just got on with things after that, and now I can hardly even picture him. I was only six. You don't take any notice when you're that young."

"No, I know I didn't. But it's great to see you again. You here for a visit?" For some reason I couldn't stop smiling. I couldn't stop looking at her legs either, which wasn't like me at all.

"Sad news, I'm afraid. Gran died, and she left me and Mum her house. We're both at a, er, crossroads in our lives, so we've done a worryingly mad thing." Helen rubbed at the cobbles with her white Converse and lowered her head until her curls covered most of her face.

"Don't tell me. You split from your long-term partner, your mum retired early, and you've both been feeling lost. You decided to pack in your job, and rather than sell the property and split the money, you're going to move in together, renovate it, and live back here where you were born."

Helen's eyes were wide as she lifted her head. "How did you know that?"

"I'm good at figuring things out," I admitted, and I am. "That, and this is a small town and you should never forget that everything you do will be news before you even realise you've done it. I bet you get your milk delivered at six twenty-three, right?"

"Ha, you had me there for a minute, Bran. And how do you know about the milk?"

"I'm a local now, and I know the round. Same as everyone else. So, you're here to stay?" I asked, feeling a surge of hope and unable to stop my stupid grin.

"Sure am. Mum's already going potty moaning about all the hippies and incense. But she isn't fooling me. The last few years she's taken much more interest in pagan things. Crystals, fortune telling, herbs, even spells, if you can believe it. She wants to be a witch, I think, but won't admit it. I think it's just because she's been thinking more about Dad and how he was obsessed, and losing Gran brought it all back. The novelty is wearing off though, but yes, we're staying. We can't go back because we both sold up. A new chapter."

"A new chapter," I agreed.

"And I'm surprised to see you here," said Helen. "You moved away, didn't you?"

"Can we talk about this another time?" I asked, trying to avoid the conversation like I always did.

"Sure." Helen frowned at my abruptness, but then something must have clicked, probably recalling what she'd been told maybe by her Gran when she came to visit, or through the grapevine, and she blurted, "Bran, I'm so sorry. That was very insensitive. I haven't been back for a good few years. Gran always came up to ours, but she did tell me. There was always so much gossip, and I just didn't pay much attention. Forgive me?"

"There's nothing to forgive. Let's catch up properly soon. What do you say?" Wow, was I really being this brazen? She was nice, and it would just be a chat.

"Sure, and oh, don't suppose you know any builders, do you? We need major renovations done, and I don't know where to start."

"You've come to the right person. Drop by the shop this afternoon a little before five, then come back to mine."

"What? Wow, you don't hang about, do you?" she said, smiling but looking rather put upon.

I forced my blush down, reminding myself I was a guy in his thirties, not some kid, and misunderstandings were no big deal. "Sorry, I should have worded that better. I meant I live with my brother and cousin and they're builders. I help them out now and then too. Best work you'll find in town. Come check them out, have a chat, and maybe you can arrange for the work to be done."

"Oh, right. That sounds great."

Did I notice disappointment there? Did she wish I meant something different? "I'm the shop at the bottom of the street. No, I'm not a shop, I'm a man. I own the shop. Bran's Dream. If you can't make it, that's fine." I shrugged, super cool.

Helen laughed, which I think was good. "You have your own shop? That's brilliant. And I'll be there. Now, can I say hello to your dog?"

I'd totally forgotten about Kale. I turned to him and took the death vibes he was sending me without complaint. "Remember I'm here, do you? She's nice, but stop acting like such a wally. And yes, she can say hello." Kale stood, making Helen gasp at his size. She was about five foot four, so when he raised his head she had to reach up to stroke it.

"Who's a handsome boy?" she asked, rubbing his ears.

"Me?" I blurted, wondering what the hell was wrong with me.

"You wish," she snickered, then bent a little and whispered in Kale's ear. She turned to me and said, "See you later, Mr. Handsome."

Kale and I watched her walk down the street until I felt the vibe.

"What?" I asked, turning to him.

"You're thinking she has a nice bum, aren't you?"

"Don't be daft," I laughed.

"Suit yourself, 'Mr. Handsome', who isn't wondering about her tan lines at all." With a swish of his tail, Kale trotted into Lovely Buns, the best bakery either side of the England/Wales border.

I followed in his wake, unsure what to feel, pangs of guilt stabbing at me like gnomes tugging on fishing lines in my guts.

Kale turned at the doorway, face sympathetic. "It's okay to like her. Don't feel bad about it."

I nodded, knowing he was right.

Lovely Buns

The bakery was rammed with locals and tourists alike. Everyone in the area knows about Lovely Buns and the outstanding offerings Humbert, the proprietor, sells. People come from far and wide to buy bread of all manner, from sourdough to the more herbal variety that locals know is the real deal, and tourists can't wait to sample because they either think it's funny, or have an open mind and hope it will help with what ails them. Humbert offers loaves, rolls, burger buns, pies, pasties, oggies, and that's it. No cakes, no fancy quiche, and there isn't an olive in sight as he detests them and believes everyone else should too.

He has one rule, and you had better not break it if you want to pay his extortionate prices.

"No Loud," reads the six-foot wide banner hung behind the counter, where he serves strictly from eight to one six days a week.

As we entered the hushed interior, almost like entering a library, the murmurs and warmth of the bakery enveloped me in its pleasant spell. Even tourists keep their voices low, almost reverential, picking up on the unmistakable vibe that this is a place of worship at the altar of the humble grain.

Nobody shouted, nobody jostled for position, nobody so much as raised their voice to question the monastic atmosphere that cuddled each and every customer. It makes many dizzy as they leave and the regular world slaps them in the face like a whack with a shovel full of disappointment that the sense of wellbeing isn't permanent.

I nodded to the huge man behind the counter. He smiled, then said softly to his customer in a deep baritone, "Thank you. Come again." He must say it hundreds of times a day.

Kale and I stood in line the same as always. No special treatment here. The large bakery was warm, yeasty, and akin to snuggling under the covers on a winter's night. You just can't feel glum in here.

The line moved at a decent clip—Humbert is a professional and his movements are precise, not an ounce of effort wasted. Not that he has to do much moving. He mostly stays rooted to the spot, his massive, tightly muscled, wiry frame able to reach for produce, paper bags, the till, and the ever-present card reader without him having to move his legs.

Every time a customer paid, I watched the familiar interference around Humbert like a bad TV signal readjusting. One moment there stood what many would call a giant, six foot six of lean, large-foreheaded, massive-handed baker. The next Humbert was his true self. A giant of the truest kind. Eight foot nine, limbs akin to gnarled oak, hands larger than any loaf, his back hunched, his head rubbing the dark spot on the ceiling.

As his happiness subsided, he stuttered back to his regular form, only to repeat the same thing as he gave his thanks to the customer and his till receipts marched higher.

Of course, most visitors can't see this. They just see a large, somewhat gangly man of indeterminate age, but they know there's something different about the gentle giant so act accordingly. Sometimes you'd get a whoop from a visiting witch or wizard, a knowing nod from a druid, or a wide-eyed stare from someone drawn to our town without them understanding why, gifts emerging and then trying to discover what was happening. And, of course, plenty of kids point and tell their parents the man is a giant.

People like me, though, born and bred in a world where magic is known to be real, we see the truth and basically take it for granted. When this is what you have always known, it just becomes the norm.

"What will have?" asked Humbert when it was our turn.

"Hey Humbert. Two oggies please."

Kale barked.

"Fine, make it three." I turned to Kale and warned him, "You do know how much these cost, right?"

"I know, but you can afford it."

He was right of course, but still, you have to watch the pennies if you want the pounds to take care of themselves. Sometimes I sound so old, even to myself.

Humbert leaned to his left, grabbed three oggies in one mighty hand, stuffed them expertly into the paper bags, then placed them on the counter while his other hand reached out and wrote the order on my tab.

"You pay next Friday. Is month end."

"Sure thing, Humbert. Later." With a wave, I turned to exit.

"Shouldn't be allowed," said a woman in the middle of the queue, scrunching up her face.

One look at her told me she wasn't nice. Her aura was off, full of spite. I said nothing though, because I was still in such a good mood after meeting Helen.

"It's disgusting," she told the woman she was with, who had the grace to look embarrassed.

"Who talk?" came the almost whisper of Humbert.

The room was deathly silent as everyone looked at the woman. I smiled at Kale, knowing what was coming. It was petty, but sometimes people need taking down a peg or two. Sometimes they even become better people for the realisation that being pleasant is far more rewarding than being obnoxious.

"I did," she said, defiant, her voice loud.

Humbert pointed at the sign behind him. He hates loud noise; it messes with his happy place. "Is mean. Kale is nice dog. Bran is friend. My shop. My rules."

"But it's a dog. It's dirty. I don't want to eat contaminated food."

There was a gasp from the half dozen or so regulars, and puzzled looks from everyone else.

"You dirty. Not dog. Have foul mouth and mean heart. Out!" Humbert spoke softly, the words more powerful for it.

The woman's mouth opened and closed like a landed fish. She turned beetroot red and then puffed out her chest, grabbed her friend, and said, "Come on, we're leaving." To a quiet round of applause, they dashed out and scampered away down the street.

Kale and I nodded again to Humbert then left, eager to get our lunch where it needed to be. In our empty bellies.

"Don't let that woman get to you," I told Kale.

"She was dumb. Full of anger. She didn't mean it, she just didn't know any better."

"You're more understanding than I am. I can't stand people like that."

"Can I have my lunch, please?" Kale eyed the bags greedily, drool hanging halfway to the cobbles.

"Sure," I chuckled. "Sorry, just thinking."

"About round bottoms in tiny shorts?" he asked, head cocked to the side.

"She had lovely legs too," I mused.

"And it's okay to notice. It's not like you haven't been on any dates. She's not the first woman since your wife died."

"You always have been blunt. And I appreciate it, buddy. I know I've seen a few women, but it never works out. I always feel like there's something missing."

"That certain spark? An intensity? Butterflies in your stomach?"

"Exactly! You know what I mean."

"Actually, I don't. Zero idea. In case you've forgotten, I'm a dog. I sniff bums, lots of them. And if one female doesn't run away, I class that as a win. No fuss, no hassle."

"Sounds ideal," I sighed.

"Trust me, it's awesome." Kale winked, then nudged my hand.

"Let's go to the square."

We wandered further up the the hill. I was sweating by the time we reached the top, then took a right and a left, then sat in the tiny market square where the last of the daily stalls were packing up. It's stupid, but there's some old law about the market having to be gone by twelve, and nobody has bothered to repeal it. All part of the mystery of Little Hope. A sense of urgency never hindered a tourist parting with their money.

We sat on a bench and munched contentedly on our oggies. Close to the Welsh border, it's a staple in these parts. Think Cornish pasty but twice the size, with flakier pastry, leek, potato, and beef. Kale made short work of his two. A few mouthfuls and he was done.

"Stop staring at me," I told him.

"Can't help it. Still hungry."

"You're always hungry."

"I'm a big dog. And being a familiar is exhausting. Talking and thinking like a human is very taxing, you know."

"You might have mentioned it. But you don't think like a human. You think like a smart dog."

"True. And have I really mentioned how taxing it is before?"

"Yes, usually around lunchtime," I laughed. "Go run around or something. Stretch those long legs of yours."

"Tired. Don't wanna."

"Then have a doze. Soak up the heat."

Kale curled up beside me and was soon dozing off his lunch. He's a real soft fella, with a heart of gold. He loves people, adores sleeping, and doesn't have a bad bone in his body. Not that it stops him guarding me and his friends with a ferocious intensity bordering on the psychotic. Irish Wolfhounds are renowned for their obedience, their laid back attitude, and their deep bond with humans. He's the epitome of a proud ancient breed that has integrated with those that have the space and can afford to keep their vast tummies full.

My companion has all those traits and one other very special one. He is my familiar. My guardian angel, if you will. He keeps my spirits high, my mind busy, my abilities bubbling away. Not that they are anything spectacular, and my time away from the heart of magic has certainly meant they've waned. Most importantly, far more precious a gift than magic, Kale makes me certain that love still exists in the world.

It has been said that just staring into the innocent eyes of a dog calms you, makes you experience love, and I don't doubt it for a moment. Being with Kale is beyond special, and I love him like a brother. Sometimes more, because he never leaves socks on the bathroom floor. Sure, he shredded the odd denim jacket when he was a puppy, and there was that thing with the slippers that took a while to sort out, and he did once try to eat Standin', although the daft gnome had it coming, but above all else, he is my friend. You can't put a price on that, as the man who once tried to steal Kale can certainly testify to. Dogs like Kale are big business, literally, and when a man tried to take him he found himself very swiftly known forever more as Stumpy.

Kale opened a lazy eye in warning and told me, "Look out, here comes trouble," then promptly fell back to sleep.

I was tempted to feign a doze myself, but before I had a chance, the local moaner, although, to be fair, there are quite a few, was upon me.

"Ah, Bran, just the fellow I wanted to see."

"What can I do for you, Snodgrass?" Blast your brains? Slap you around the head with a willing gnome? Tell you to shove it and stop talking to me?

Instead, I mustered a fake smile from deep down and waited for the complaining to begin.

"Did you hear the news?" asked Snodgrass, eyes gleaming.

"What news?"

"About that poor fellow falling to his death. Terrible, just terrible." Snodgrass leered, excited by something dramatic happening in Little Hope.

"I heard. I met him and his wife earlier."

"Really? Did he look sick? Like he might collapse?"

"No, he seemed fine. Look, what do you want? I'm busy."

"You have to do something about that damn Outdoors Is Lovely shop. Stupid name, by the way, don't you think?" He got right up in my face, red-rimmed eyes never blinking, like being observed by a snake.

"Back it up a little, please." His breath was sour; Snodgrass seems to live on cabbage and greasy sausages.

"Oh, sorry, didn't realise I was so close." He knew, but he still always does it.

"I like the name. It's quirky."

"Quirky? Hmm, I suppose it is. But I don't like it." He smoothed down his black trousers and brushed a shower of dandruff from the lapels of his jacket, then wiped his forehead with a red polka dot handkerchief. "My, will this heat never end?"

"You should embrace it. Get some air to your legs. Try sandals instead of shoes. And you don't need a jacket."

"I have standards to uphold. No Snodgrass has ever worn shorts and I'm not willing to start now." He glared up at the clear sky as if daring the sun to continue shining. "Now, about the outdoor clothing shop."

"Look," I sighed, "I've told you already, same as everyone else has told you, it's nothing to do with me. Anyone can open a shop if they have rent money. And it's brought extra business to the town. Half the tourists that arrive are here to go walking as well as for the ambiance, and most of them aren't prepared. Freddy is good for business. He's a nice guy, and he pays his rent on time according to Captain. There's nothing I can do."

"You could have a word with him. Tell Captain we don't want the likes of Freddy here. He's not local."

"Half the people who live here aren't local. It's the way of the world now. If it wasn't for outsiders settling here, the town would be half the size. Lots of the younger generation want to go off and see the world, same as I did, same as many others, so it's good we get fresh blood in. And the other races like gnomes, the giants, the, er, darker elements, are they outsiders too?"

"What? Of course not! I didn't mean it like that. I welcome our supernatural brothers and sisters with open arms, but there must be limits."

"As I said, Freddy pays his rent on time. I like him. And his shop is good for the town. You need to embrace his approach, maybe update your own shoe shop."

"Snodgrass' Shoes has been on Wizard's Way for three hundred years! From humble beginnings as cobblers, our family worked hard to become pillars of this community. And now this outsider comes with his newfangled walking boots at ridiculous prices and he's taking my business." Snodgrass wiped his brow again, then blew his nose into the damp handkerchief.

"We all have to compete with each other. It's the way of business. You were the only place to buy boots for a long time, but now you have competition. That's how commerce works."

"Yes, yes, I understand that. But he's so expensive. Why do people buy from him?"

"That's something you'll have to figure out for yourself."

"I just don't understand it," he muttered, then wandered off without saying goodbye, eager to accost someone else.

"He's such a mean old man," said Kale once he was gone.

"Just an old wizard set in his ways." Kale raised his head to look at me. "Fine, and he's mean-spirited and thinks he has the right to run the town because his family has been here so long."

"Yours have been here longer."

"Tell him that. He hates that Captain owns more property than him. Which is something I've always wondered. How come Captain didn't own the houses we bought? He's got the money. He could have snapped them up."

"You're so dumb sometimes."

"Huh?"

"Ask him. It's pretty obvious."

"I will."

Snodgrass is harmless enough, but he's one of those people who never crack a smile and is always sour, like the world owes him something. When Freddy came to town, and stayed, and then opened a shop selling all manner of outdoor gear, he nearly blasted the place to cinders.

It isn't difficult to understand why people prefer to shop there. Would you rather go to a musty old shop with outdated stock where the carpet is threadbare and the lights flicker, with a sour old man right up in your face as you look around, or a bright, airy, modern shop full of the latest in designer comfort, where you can get free drinks and cake and have a laugh with the utterly flamboyant owner who has real-life puppies running around? It's a no-brainer. Freddy attracts a lot of curious visitors. He's been in magazines, has coverage online, apparently, and add in a magical twist and it's no wonder Snodgrass' nose is put out of joint.

I people-watched until the hour was up, content to soak up the atmosphere, marvel at the clothes some tourists wore, and giggle as no end of them wandered around with devices held up in the air as they tried in vain to get a signal. We even have signs at the various entry points to town. *We Have no Internet Signal. That Means no Wi-Fi! Oh, and no Phone Signal Either!!!*

Sometimes our town takes things rather literally, and we never use a single word when a long sentence is an option. Those in charge of such signs are also big on exclamation marks. They seem to think it makes people take notice. It doesn't. Anyone who sees the signs thinks it's a joke. Where doesn't have a mobile signal or internet access? A place where there are more supernatural or connected people than regular folk, that's where. We play havoc with tech.

Lunchtime was over soon enough, so I woke Kale and we sauntered back down Wizard's Way, then I unlocked the shop, greeting those waiting outside, and had a profitable few hours.

I was distracted all afternoon, felt nervous and antsy, and kept thinking about poor Albert and his wife, and my conversation with Calum. Had I done the right thing? Had I said enough? But Calum said it was an accident, so that was the end of the matter, surely?

Most of all, I couldn't get Helen out of my mind. I'd heard about her gran, but hadn't known her that well. Even in a small town, you never get to truly know everyone. Some appreciate their privacy, like me, and her gran was the same. Helen and I were close as kids, but she'd moved away so long ago that the memory faded until it was hardly there at all. Seeing her didn't bring much back. I was simply too young. What I did know was that I'd love to get to know her better this time around.

Would she feel the same? Was I asking too much of someone who'd just moved back? Did she have even an inkling what she was letting herself in for? I doubted it. She might have been to visit her gran over the years, and I couldn't believe I'd never seen her, so would have no doubt been regaled with many a witchy story, but the reality is always very different from the stories. If she even believed at all. Maybe she didn't. It wouldn't matter. Her gran comes from a long line of witches and wizards, so even if she had no gifts as of yet, now she was back they'd surface no matter what she believed. Little Hope would see to that.

Woman!

"You came," I beamed, turning as I caught Helen's scent on the early evening breeze. It was like walking through an apple orchard.

"Yes, sorry I'm late. You're locking up, but at least I made it."

"It's not a problem," I told her, turning the key in the lock then smiling. "You look nice. Did you do something to your hair since earlier?" It took me many years to realise that giving heartfelt compliments to people is a nice thing to do and always appreciated. People like to feel good about themselves.

"Just washed it. And got changed. It's very hot."

"Smells of apples. With a hint of lemon. And I'm getting chocolate. Sorry, but I have a keen sense of smell. All Fairfield's do. Ugh, I'm blathering."

"It's nice you noticed." Helen was in good spirits, and she smiled even as I wittered on, which was definitely a good sign.

"Would you like a coffee at mine? You can meet the others and see about getting a quote for the work."

"That's why I'm here," she said. "And to spend time with Mr. Handsome. At least according to him."

"I was just joking," I said lamely.

"Maybe, but you are handsome. I love the long hair."

I guess Helen knew about compliments, too.

Kale led while Helen and I chatted about this and that as we made our way to the car. Often, I'd walk to work, but I'd brought stock in early this morning so drove instead.

At the house, I asked, "Do you mind just waiting here for one minute. I haven't warned the others, not that I mean warn them about you, and I just want to make sure they haven't made a mess. Sorry."

"That's okay." Helen nodded, so I dashed inside.

"You can't bring a woman in here," gasped Forest, eyes darting around the living room.

"Why not?" I asked, amused by his panic, and the armful of socks, magazines, and old games cartridges he was now trying, and failing, to keep bundled in his arms.

"You haven't given us notice. Housemates need a warning about guests. So they can prepare."

"Prepare what? The place looks nice. I'm the one who should be nervous."

"Oh, is she hot?"

"Cool it. She's nice, and just back in town, so be friendly. But not too friendly," I warned.

"Whatever you say." Forest grinned; I knew that grin meant trouble.

With a wag of my finger, I went to invite Helen inside.

"So, this is Forest, my brother," I said, waving a hand in his general direction.

"Hey," said Forest.

"Hi. So you really are called Forest?"

"Yep. Our folks are proper hippy types. They figured it would make me more magical. Commune with the trees, all that jazz." Forest waved it away, then put a hand to his mouth. "Not that I am a you-know-what. No, ha, how silly."

"Not that you are a what?" asked Helen, beyond confused.

"A what?" asked Forest, dark tanned face screwed up in utter confusion."

"You said not that you are a you-know-what. But I wasn't thinking of anything. What aren't you?"

"Oh, right. Loads of things. I'm not a porpoise, or a cat. But I meant I wasn't a wizard."

"Why would I think you were? Because you're called Forest?"

"No, because I told you they thought it would make me magical. But I'm not. See, can't even cast a spell." Forest waved his hand at the pile of junk mail on the Ercol coffee table and a gust of wind knocked them onto the floorboards.

"Oops," I said hurriedly, dashing over and picking them up. "Didn't see them there." I glared at Forest, then was relieved when I heard the final member of the household clomp into the living room.

"Roger!" we both exclaimed, making Helen jump. Poor thing looked bewildered, and it wasn't surprising. Despite hoping for the best, it was a total disaster. Forest never was able to keep his mouth shut. I was acting weird too. I knew I was, but couldn't seem to help it.

"This is Roger the Lodger. He's, er, the lodger."

"I wish you guys would stop calling me that," sulked Roger.

"You aren't the lodger? And hi, I'm Helen." They shook hands.

"No. I live here."

"That's what lodgers do, isn't it? Live in a house?"

"I mean I live here just like them. Nice to meet you. Why are you guys looking so weird? And why are you standing in a line?"

"Because we're introducing ourselves," said Forest. "Being polite."

"I did meet Bran earlier, remember?" said Helen, smiling nervously. "I came here with him."

"You look suspicious," noted Roger, studying Forest. "This the magic thing again?"

"No, course not," I said, shaking my head.

"What magic thing?" asked Helen.

"Nothing. Roger was just messing around, weren't you, Roger?" I said, nodding.

"What is with you? You got a problem with your head? I keep telling you, nobody cares. Nobody ever has. Nobody ever will."

"About the magic thing?" prompted Helen.

"Yes. They like to act secretive and pretend they're normal. But they aren't. Look at them. Pair of misfits."

"So, as I was saying, Roger the Lodger lives here too. Sorry about the mess. Some of us are more untidy than others." I gave Forest a look; he knew who I was talking about.

"I'm trying, but it's hard to adjust. I'm not used to all the stuff."

"You lived in the woods for like a month, and you hated it," I told him.

"It was longer than that. And I didn't hate it. But there was no electricity. Couldn't see a thing at night."

"And it was years ago," added Roger.

"I need to get out of this place," I sighed, knowing I was right where I needed to be.

"Just to clear things up," said Roger. "I am not the lodger. I live here same as everyone else. We all pay our share, we have equal rights, and I'm your cousin!"

"You were last in. That means you're the lodger," Forest told him. "We all agreed."

"I didn't!"

"Roger, everyone has to obey the house rules," I laughed.

"It's been years!"

"Are you guys always this mad?" asked Helen, laughing but clearly understandably overwhelmed.

"No, sometimes it's worse," I sighed.

"And I have to say, I'm amazed at your home. It's so clean. So neat and tidy. I expected, er..."

"You expected a pigsty because three men live together, didn't you?" I asked, wagging my finger. "For shame."

"I did," Helen admitted. "It's lovely. A real sixties Scandinavian feel. Very minimal and the opposite of the shop."

"The shop is styled how people expect it to look. It helps them relax. Come on, I'll make a cuppa."

I led the way into the kitchen, the one place we keep properly spotless. Three men in a house means there is bound to be a struggle for space, but the rules are clear. You use something, you wash it up or put it in the dishwasher.

"I need to phone Mum," said Helen. "I forgot to tell her I'd be late back. She's super stressed with the move."

"Use the landline. It's over there." I pointed to the beige phone on the wall.

"I keep forgetting about the signal, or lack of it. How can you manage without internet or your mobile?"

I shrugged. "You get used to it. You just have to be organised. Actually, I prefer it. It's liberating."

"You do? Seriously? But I have to drive half an hour to check my email. I can't look anything up online, and I'm already getting withdrawal from social media."

"And you're feeling better for it, right?" I asked, smiling.

"Yes," she admitted, trying to look sad, but her eyes twinkled and her little dimples made her look super cute. Cute? When was the last time I used that word? Maybe never. I was a grown man, not a lovesick teenager. "I've got loads more free time, I'm sleeping better as I don't check my phone, and I'm happier because no social media means I'm not getting annoyed or depressed when I see what other people are doing. Why do we obsess over what other people are eating? It's nuts."

"I felt exactly the same way at first. Then you just forget about it. Haven't even bothered to take my laptop to get a signal for over three months now. There's no point."

"This place really is a different world, isn't it? I can't believe they haven't found a way to get us connected, though."

I shrugged. "Just because of where we are. Right on the edge, and our little town is special." I held off saying it was because of the magic here, that the supernatural community negated technology, and it had snowballed. The more like me who came here, the worse the problem got, until eventually all modern technology just stopped working. Except card readers. All the shops accept cards as payment. Supernaturals may play havoc with tech, but when it comes to earning a living, spells make sure everyone still gets paid.

"It is special, isn't it? I'm glad I returned. Although I still feel like an idiot for running home with my mother. It's like holding up a huge banner saying I couldn't cope in the big, bad world outside. Talking of which. What's with the signs at the main road? That's a lot of exclamation marks."

"Nothing wrong with that," I told her. "Coming home, I mean. Not exclamation marks! Ugh! Now it sounds like everything I say ends with one!"

"Argh, stop it! Look, now I'm doing it! Is it contagious?"

"I think it might be," I chuckled. "Phew, the spell seems to have waned. But look, lots of people come home for one reason or another. That's what Little Hope is. It's home to so many of us."

"Oh, Bran, I'm so sorry. I didn't mean it like that. I heard about your wife, and it was just terrible. I never meant to suggest you came running home because you couldn't cope."

"I didn't for years. Lost the plot, got fat, never went out, quit my stupid job in that ridiculous place. Then I got better and realised that I loved this town. So I came home and haven't been happier."

"I think I'm going to feel the same way. It's been great to see you, Bran. It's been too long. It's unbelievable that we haven't got together since we were kids. I've been back lots of times over the years. But I guess you weren't here anyway. Doesn't matter, we're both here now."

"It's great to see you too. Let me make the coffee while you use the antique means of communication."

Helen went to make her call. I couldn't help checking out her nice bum, then felt a pang of guilt, like I was betraying Emily. Was I? No, it was silly, and this was the first time I'd felt like this for so long it just came as a shock. Helen was nice, and to hell with it, yes, she was cute.

I giggled to myself as I made the drinks. Cute! I really was reverting to being a teenager. It felt good. Liberating. Like I was finally becoming whole. But it was still too soon to think about taking it further than casual dating, wasn't it? And why would I even think she liked me? What was wrong with me? I had butterflies in my stomach. I suppressed another giggle.

"You're smitten," tittered Forest like a shy schoolgirl.

"Am not," I hissed, glancing at Helen and waving to her like an utter moron.

"You just waved at her. What is wrong with you?"

"He's in love," Roger told him.

"Am not. And will you guys stop messing about? She'll hear you."

"Sorry bruv, you know we're just joking about." Forest studied me with his pale blue eyes. Eyes that mean he never has a problem with dating. The tan and muscles don't hurt either.

"I think it's nice," said Roger. "It's about time you got yourself a fine woman."

"Hey, I've met a few since I've been back."

"And then you make an excuse and break it off," Forest reminded me.

"Do not."

"Do too," said Roger, elbowing Forest in the ribs as they both laughed.

"You're enjoying watching me squirm, aren't you?"

"Maybe a little," admitted Forest. "If I can't tease my little brother, then what's the point of having one?"

"I'm not exactly little. It's only two years difference. What's your excuse?" I asked Roger.

"I enjoy it," he shrugged. "Seriously though, she's nice. And that bum. Oh boy. How come we've never met her?"

"She moved away when she was six. Her gran stayed, but her mum didn't enjoy coming back so they hardly ever visited. Her gran visited them."

"Makes sense," said Roger. "Think she's loaded? Will this be a big job?" He rubbed his hands together.

"Don't you dare take advantage of her."

"When have we ever done that?" asked Forest. "We have a great reputation as we never overcharge, do proper work, and only have six tea breaks a day."

"Plus lunch," I reminded him.

"Course plus lunch," he said, looking perplexed.

"And morning coffee break," I added.

"You gotta have coffee to see you through the rest of the morning," said Roger.

"And you have an afternoon snack break."

"Yeah, but that includes one of the tea breaks," said Roger.

"No it doesn't," said Forest.

"Oh."

"Look, if you get the work, just take it easy, okay?"

"You mean slack off? No way," protested Forest. "We work hard."

"I mean take it easy on Helen, and especially her mum. I think she'll be finding it hard adjusting to our town."

"You mean all the nutjobs and freaks?" asked Roger, grinning like the idiot he sometimes is.

"No, I mean to all the kindly people just going about their business and never interfering in other people's lives." Both of them gawped at me, then we laughed. Chance would be a fine thing. "Look, I need to talk to you both. Did you hear about the man who died?"

"We heard," said Forest. "Poor guy."

"I met him and his wife earlier. We chatted, and some things were said."

Forest and Roger leaned in close, eager for gossip. We all turned as Helen entered the room, so I whispered, "I'll tell you later."

"What were you guys laughing at? Not the new girl who's finding it strange being back and trying to adjust to the, er, atmosphere?" Helen smiled; they really were some serious dimples.

"Of course not," said Roger. "We were saying it must be hard getting used to the freaks and nutjobs, though."

"You were," I reminded him. "Everyone's different here. I like it."

"Me too," said Forest."

"Yeah, so do I," admitted Roger. "Not that me and Forest know any different. It's always been home for us. Whenever we go anywhere else, it seems so normal. So boring. There's no magic."

We exchanged a glance, but Helen clearly didn't take it that way. Or did she?

"So you guys believe in magic?"

She obviously did take it that way.

"Look, I'm sure your gran filled you with tales about this place, and about herself and your ancestors. You left when you were little, and from what I've heard your mum kept you away from anything even remotely magical, right?" asked Forest.

"She never wanted to talk about it. Only Gran ever did, and Mum was never happy about it. Dad was the one who she said was really into the magical side of things. I never knew if she was making up stories or not."

"Well, a lot of what your gran told you is true. It's nothing weird, just different."

"Forest's right," I told her. "Nobody goes blasting fireballs at evil sorcerers or anything, but—"

"There was that one time when Captain blew up that airplane," said Roger.

"But magic is real. We don't hide it, we don't pretend it doesn't exist, but most of it is herbs and mild spells and that kind of thing. Oh, and talking dogs and cats. The usual."

"That's all right then," she laughed. When we didn't laugh along with her, she frowned then began to look uncomfortable. "Guys, just because I'm the new girl doesn't mean you have to make fun of me. Come on."

"We're just messing about, Helen. But seriously, keep an open mind. Little Hope is different."

"Yeah, the town of Little Hope."

"Aha, that's where you're wrong. Look," I told her, "you can think of it either way. Either it's a town of little hope, or it means there is still a little hope. We like to think of it as a positive thing. There is always hope. Always Little Hope."

"I like that. Now, where's my coffee?" She smiled. Those dimples again.

"Can we have coffee too?" asked Roger.

"No, you can both go to your rooms and stay there until Helen wants to talk business with you two clowns."

Everyone looked at me, and I knew it was a lost cause.

"Is he always like this?" asked Helen, amused by my outburst, and clearly unsure if I was serious. I was, but the guys knew they had a chance to wind me up, so there was no escape.

"Only around hot women," said Forest with a wink to Helen.

"I'll have you know, Forest, that in the modern world we don't talk about the opposite, or the same, sex like that." Helen stared him down until he looked away.

"Sorry."

"Ha, gotcha! So you think I'm hot?"

"Yes," chorused me and Forest.

"Not my type," said Roger.

Helen turned to him and asked, "What is?"

Roger shrugged. "Pretty much anyone with a beard."

"He does like a beard," I told Helen.

"Loves them," agreed Forest.

Helen frowned. "You like women with beards?"

"No, men with beards," Roger explained.

"Oh, right. That makes much more sense."

"And he pulls all the time. Always off out with some guy," said Forest with another wink.

"Stop winking at her," Roger told him. "Nobody likes that."

"You don't mind, do you?" asked Forest, winking again.

"It is a bit much. Is it a facial tic?"

Forest was crestfallen and told me, "I'm going off her."

"Liar," I laughed. I turned to Helen and said, "Forest has about as much practise with, er, nice women as I do. He got divorced four years ago, was married since his early twenties, so we're both, er..."

"Clumsy, always say the wrong thing, and a bit over-eager," added Roger helpfully.

"I was about to say, we're both rather cautious and not the best at reading the signs," I told him. "Not that I'm suggesting you were, you know. Ugh, let's have the coffee."

We sat in the living room and chatted while we drank. Helen filled us in on her background, how she'd hated her job and jumped at the chance to move back here even though it felt like a leap into the unknown. She wanted adventure, and little did she know it but she'd get more than she bargained for in this place.

There was no boyfriend or husband, just a long-term now ex, and she'd been single for a while now. Good news for me. Not that I was pleased to hear about the bad break-up.

"Helen, give me your opinion on this, will you?" Forest dashed into the kitchen like an eager kid, then returned with his box of spices. Roger and I groaned.

"Don't do it," I warned.

"Shut it, Bran. I want her opinion. You should invite her over for curry night. We can get to know each other better." I shot him daggers; he grinned as he knew he was making me squirm. Last thing I wanted was a date with my housemates present.

"What is it?" Helen's eyes twinkled as she looked at the large tin.

"I've been experimenting with Sri Lankan curries. I've made the mix and I want your opinion. Just take a sniff. See what you think."

"If you value your sinuses, you won't," I advised her. "The curries taste great, but the spices knock your socks off."

"I love Sri Lankan food," Helen told him.

"Great." Forest opened a small tin and held it under her nose.

Helen took a tentative sniff, then a larger one. She waved Forest away as she gasped for air and spluttered, "That's... very strong. Isn't it meant to be less, er, pungent?"

"I told you," chuckled Roger. "You put too much chilli in it."

"I did not. It's meant to be a spicy one. Well, what do you think?"

"I'm sure it will be lovely." Helen's eyes were watering and her nose was very red, and then, with a violent judder, she sneezed.

Calm as you like, Forest put his tin on the coffee table, Roger and I put down our mugs, and Kale came over and sniffed the cute bunny rabbit sitting on the sofa. The rabbit's ears twitched as Kale licked the tiny pink nose, then he returned to his bed. He'd seen it all before.

"Um, Helen, did you know that would happen?" asked Forest.

"Sometimes you are so dumb," I said.

"You are."

"Of course she didn't know. Look what you did. You turned Helen into a bunny. What was in that curry?"

"Nothing, honest. Just regular herbs and spices. No funny business," he protested, arms out.

"Must be the family magic catching up with her," I mused. I bent until I was eye to eye with Helen bunny, and whispered, "Stay calm, don't panic, and, er, don't go hopping off."

"That was so lame," said Forest.

"About as lame as you can get," agreed Roger. "Stand aside, gentlemen, I know how to cure it."

"We all know how to cure it," I told him.

"Really? How?"

"She needs to sneeze again to shift back to human form," said Forest.

"Yep," I agreed.

"Fine, but you still need to shift." Roger put the tin under the twitching rabbit's nose and said, "Take a deep sniff. Then you'll be fine." The rabbit did as instructed and sneezed.

Helen was back to being herself.

"You make a very cute bunny," I said, smiling.

"Very cute," agreed Forest.

"I could just eat you up," said Roger.

We turned to look at him as he stood there cradling Forest's precious spice tin.

"Idiot," I muttered.

"What? I didn't mean I'd eat her. You guys." Roger wandered off, then turned straight back around and handed the tin to Forest who took it to the kitchen, returning it to its rightful place.

I turned to Helen and asked, "Are you okay?"

Helen ran shaking hands through her hair and asked, "You guys aren't shocked? Why aren't you freaking out? I wish I could stop it."

"It'll settle down once the rest of your powers manifest," said Forest with a soothing voice.

"It's not that uncommon," I agreed. "Main thing is to make sure you do the second sneeze. Bet it scared you the first time, eh?"

"Ha, you bet it did. I can't believe you aren't concerned."

"I told you, this is magic town. Get used to it." I smiled at her and asked, "You want another coffee?"

"I think I better. But thank you. All of you. It's been happening for a while now and I haven't told Mum as she hates this stuff. So, it's true, my family were witches and wizards? I'm sorry I acted like I knew nothing about the magic around here. I didn't want to make a fool of myself, now look what I've done."

"Don't worry about pretending. It's understandable. But there's more to it," I said. "You're a witch too."

"I feel kinda witchy," she laughed, and there was a sultry undertone to it as she smiled at me and winked.

I gulped.

She's one really cute bunny.

Down to Business

After the second coffee, Helen settled down and asked a ton of questions she really should have already known. Her mother had done a great job of keeping much of what went on here secret, but I was amazed her gran hadn't told her more. Guess she was just following the wishes of her daughter. Not everyone likes the magical side of life, and that's fair enough. I'd turned my back on much of it when I moved away too, although I always found the time to keep my hand in a little, and returned home often enough to never lose touch.

Being back isn't without its trials, though. Family are hard to get on with all the time, and add in the risk of being turned into a toad or waking up without your feet, and let's just say it can get intense at times.

Helen seemed to be taking it all in her stride, which is more than can be said for some who simply can't handle it and leave, never to return.

They talked business for a while so I kept quiet, and I'd zoned out when Forest suddenly blurted, "Look at the time!"

Roger and I glanced at our watches, then groaned.

"I forgot," I told him.

"Me too. I thought it was Thursday," complained Roger.

"I didn't, but I still forgot."

"Other things on your mind?" asked Forest, nudging his head in Helen's direction.

"Shut up," I snapped.

"I can see you do that," giggled Helen.

"No you can't. I did it very subtly," said Forest.

"Oh, my mistake then." Helen turned to me, eyebrows raised. I shook my head, telling her without speaking that sometimes Forest was an idiot. She smiled.

"Sorry, but we have to go. It's Family Dinner Friday and we can't miss it. Shall I walk you home?"

"I think I'll be alright," laughed Helen. "But thank you."

"Why don't you invite her along?" said Roger, acting innocent.

"Yeah, introduce the new girl to the mad old Fairfields," chuckled Forest.

I glowered at them both, then turned to Helen and said, "Another time. It'll be a bit much for you at the moment. Our dads, and Captain, can be a little..."

"Utterly deranged. Annoying. Liable to stand you in a corner and quiz you until you run screaming down Wizard's Way." I glared at Forest again. He just shrugged.

"Something like that. But why not pop into the shop tomorrow? How about twelve? We could get lunch." I felt nervous even asking. What if she rejected me? Was I reading this wrong? I was a grown man, not some kid. I could handle it either way.

"Can we make it half past?"

"Sure."

"Sounds lovely. It's a date."

"It is?"

"Isn't it?"

"I hope so. But I didn't want to presume."

"So you just wanted me to come for lunch and not have a date?"

"Very funny. You got me. Stop trying to make me squirm," I grinned. I liked this woman.

"We like her," said Forest.

Roger nodded in agreement.

"Even though I turn into a bunny?"

"A cute one," I reminded her.

"See you tomorrow then?"

"Absolutely."

Helen said goodbye to Kale, which meant she was definitely a keeper, and he told me so, then I saw her to the door.

When I closed it and turned around, the guys were standing there, grinning like they'd won the National Lottery on a double rollover.

"What's wrong with your faces?" I asked, feigning innocence.

"She's awesome," said Forest. "You lucky sod. Did you see her bum?"

"Can't say I noticed."

"And those dimples," added Roger. "She's even cute as a bunny."

"Guess some of us have all the charm. Who could resist my awesome looks and amazing personality?"

The guys' smiles faded and they stared past me. I suddenly went very cold, then very hot.

I turned and saw that the letterbox was open. I bent and peered into Helen's twinkling eyes.

"Just checking," she laughed.

"Checking what?"

"That you weren't saying anything dumb, or mean, or rude about me."

"Were we?" I couldn't for the life of me recall a single word of the conversation.

"Nope, it's all good. See you tomorrow." The letterbox snapped shut. I waited several seconds, then opened the door like a ninja and poked my head around.

Helen was halfway down the street. She raised a hand and waved without looking around.

"She is so awesome," said Forest, now right beside me.

Roger's head appeared beside mine as we watched her turn the corner. "One in a million. If you blow this, then I might turn straight and ask her out myself." Forest and I gawped at him. "Joking. But I like her."

"Me too," I sighed.

"Did we say anything dumb?" I asked them.

"Does it matter? She likes us," said Forest with a little too much enthusiasm.

"Cool it. She's mine. Or, er, you know, we might have a date."

"I was just wondering."

"What?"

"Maybe she has a sister. Or what's her mum like? I am older than you."

"You have a girlfriend," I reminded him.

"I know. I'm just joking around."

Roger punched him on the arm and told us both, "Get ready. We're going to be late."

With a deep breath, we steeled ourselves for Family Dinner Friday. Which basically consists of three much older men giving the three cool kids a load of grief about anything they can think of, and much that they can't.

Family Dinner Friday

I closed the front door behind us and we walked down the steps onto the path that leads along the front garden. It's large, but nothing like the rear garden that comprises a half acre, same as each of the rest of the houses in the plot. Relatively long and narrow, it's still luxurious after living in a conventional townhouse as I did for many years.

We exited the front gate and Forest and Roger couldn't resist crossing the lane and standing back against the fence line to a field full of sheep to admire their handiwork.

"Will you look at those beauties," sighed Forest. "A true miracle."

"A thing of beauty," agreed Roger with a broad grin. They high-fived.

"You did a great job," I agreed. "I'm glad you talked me into it."

"We are too," Forest told me. "You know that. Even if you are a pain." He slapped me on the shoulder; he could never be mean for long.

"I still can't believe we own this. It's nuts. Who would have thought that the Fairfield boys would be property developers?"

"I always knew we'd do okay," sighed Roger. "And anyway, we all deserve it. We work hard, we save our money, and it was a lot of work. The houses were almost falling down. We did a good thing and saved them."

"We did," I agreed. "And thanks, you guys. I know I've said it before, but this was the right move. Even living together has worked out, right?"

"It has its moments," joked Roger.

"It's better than rattling around in a house alone," said Forest.

"Sure is. And if we ever get families, we have a ready-made home to move into."

"We just need a good woman," sighed Forest. "Although I think Bran will be kicking us out in a fortnight and asking Helen to marry him."

"Very funny. Do not," I warned, "tell the mad old men about her. I'll never hear the end of it."

"I don't need a good woman," pouted Roger.

"No, you've got a good man, which is just as nice," said Forest.

"He's a great guy, isn't he?" said Roger, a faraway look in his eyes.

"Sure is," I told him. "You going to move in together one day?"

"Maybe. But it's early days. For now, I'm happy with you guys. Sometimes."

"Liar. You love it. If you live without us, you'll have to do the laundry and make your bed. I've seen your room. It's gross," I told him.

"I do my share. But laundry. Ugh! It's such a pain. All that hanging out, then getting in, then folding, then putting on hangers. It's torture."

"I like it," said Forest. "Time to slow down and clear my head. I always thought gay guys were into clothes. You're like the opposite of gay."

"Here we go," I laughed, knowing Forest was winding Roger up, but he always bit.

"Just because I like men doesn't mean I like clothes shopping, shoes, hair gel, boy bands, pop music, or doing the laundry."

"You don't even know what Gucci is," accused Forest, getting sucked into it.

"I do. That's the, er, the perfume one, isn't it? No, wait, it's a brand of boots."

"See?" said Forest, turning to me, exasperated.

"Who cares? Roger's a bloody builder just like you, and neither of you make your bed or act like anyone else I know. And remember, not a word about Helen. I want a quiet night then a relaxing weekend."

"No chance," grinned Forest.

"Nope. We got that job on, remember? And we need to check out Helen's place, too. No rest for the wicked."

"I forgot." I didn't mind. Helping out the guys on the weekends keeps me in trim, gives me the chance to hang out with them, and we all love nosing around the old properties we get to renovate. Little Hope is full of historic buildings dating back as far as the fifteenth century. A treasure trove of information and historic artefacts for a group of locals who know exactly where to look and with the right tools for the job.

"No blabbing," I muttered.

Both smiled, then zipped their lips with their fingers. Their eyes were full of amusement, practically gagging to tell our dads and Captain about Helen. The men in our family live for two things. Magic and gossip, preferably both at the same time.

"Come on, we're cutting it close. Captain will be moaning all evening if he doesn't get his dinner on time." Forest led the way back across the road, along the rough lane, then into the garden of the property next door. Just like ours, the front is a mixture of herbs of all description and bright, happy flowers. My dad is the one with green fingers, and will spend hours dead-heading and weeding the front gardens, although he draws the line at tending anything but his own back garden.

I've inherited his green fingers, and spend a great deal of my time outside soaking up the energy, charging my magical battery so to speak, and love how it's coming along now I've got it established.

The houses are what made me finally come home. Up until that point, mine and Forest's dad, Jin, and our mother lived in the family home along with Captain, our grandfather. Our grandmother had died almost a decade ago and left him alone in the house, so our parents sold the small cottage they owned and moved in with him. It was a brave move.

Roger's father, our uncle, is estranged from Roger's mother, and after some persuasion moved in with his brother and father. They are close, like me and the guys, and the power of three makes them stronger and keeps them grounded. Same as it does for us.

But the house was a mess, and needed serious cash to bring it up to modern standards. It didn't even have radiators in all the rooms.

Then just over three years ago I got a call from Forest sounding super excited. Three of the four houses on the quiet country lane just outside the top of town were up for auction. He reckoned they'd go for a song as they were in a bad way and had been nothing but tenant farmer properties for generations. No modern kitchens, no proper heating, leaking roofs, outside toilets, and the grounds were so overgrown you could hardly even see them.

His suggestion was that we buy all three, then own one each. Me, him, and Roger. We'd be close to each other, could look after our dads and Captain, and as he and Roger were the best builders in the county, he was certain they could do the renovations for a low cost and we'd each have a true home of our own in the town we grew up in.

To say I was dubious was an understatement. Not only was it the main chunk of the money I'd got from the insurance when Emily died, but being so close to family would be claustrophobic and I knew what everyone was like. Always wanting to know your business, always poking their noses in, and always bickering. Then I admitted it to myself. That was what I missed the most about Little Hope. My family. Their madness, their nosiness, their interfering. Their love.

We'd always been close, grew up together in town, and I trusted Forest and Roger with my life, let alone my money, so I finally agreed. After all, I had nothing to lose. I was on my own after finally getting my life back together, but I despised my job, hated being so isolated in the midst of over a million people, so accepted that this was absolutely the best move to make.

And it was. Still is.

We got the houses for a ridiculously low price, and within six months Forest and Roger, along with me as I moved back down and lived with Forest while we renovated, fixed up all four houses until they were like new builds, except with soul and plenty of space.

I moved into mine, Forest into his, Roger his, and Dad, Uncle Frank, and Captain were pleased they finally had central heating. They kept the kitchen proper old school though, real wizard style, with a huge Aga that is constantly being fed by firewood and runs all year round, but they got new cupboards and are like pigs in the proverbial excrement.

It was mad, beyond mad, and I had my doubts about it working out, but work out it has. So much so, that within a month of living so close, Forest and I realised we should live together. We'd always been super close, same as with Roger who's like our other brother, so Forest moved in and rented out his place. He paid me rent, although I told him I didn't need the money, but he insisted. Then Roger came over and admitted that even though he'd pretended he wanted his own space, he would rather live with the guys. So he moved in too. Forever known as the lodger.

We agreed that whenever we felt it right they could move back out, and there would be no hard feelings. Apart from that the rules are simple, and because we are so alike it has never been an issue. Keep the house tidy, do what you want in your own room. We even have a cleaning rota, and we stick to it. After all, we aren't kids. We're men in our thirties with plenty of history behind us. We've loved, we've lost, we've picked up the pieces. But our dads, and Captain, are another story entirely.

They've been part of Little Hope for as long as anyone can remember, and they're known by everyone and get the gossip. Especially Captain. What he says goes, always has, always will, never mind he's in his eighties. The men in our family, and women by blood, live long lives. Some might say too long, but I hope Grandad lives forever. Maybe with less attitude and grump, but I love him regardless.

I was tempted to stop the guys and talk about Sheila's husband and what had happened, but what was there to tell? And besides, we really were running late and the trouble we'd be in simply meant it wasn't worth risking. And truthfully, I didn't know what to say beyond that something didn't feel right about the whole situation. It wasn't that I believed Sheila was guilty, but the death had my stomach in knots. "Behave," I warned, as I opened the front door to what may as well have been another world.

We dutifully took our flip-flops or clogs off, then slapped our bare feet on the original Georgian tiles as we walked past the stairs down the hall. The air was thick with the heady scent of three aged men, generations of hearty meals, and the unmistakable pungent mix of herbal remedies they refuse to give up making.

No amount of fresh paint, new plaster, modern kitchen gadgets, or posh central heating can disguise the odours that have sunk so deeply into the fabric of the building they act like magical mortar. I glanced into the spacious living room on the left where the stove was burning low. Captain was sitting in his chair, eyes glued to the TV as he watched his favourite show of all time, The X-Files. He watches an episode every single day at precisely six thirty. Once he's finished them in order, he starts again. I know the scripts better than the back of my hand, and I'm the most clueless about the show. Captain loves to tell you about it, and he makes us watch as often as possible. It's why dinner is at seven thirty—the rest of us get some peace before the patriarch joins us.

"Oh boy, can't wait," yapped Kale as he bounded into the living room.

"It's half over already," I laughed, same as I always did.

"Doesn't matter. I've seen it before," he said, eyes on the screen as he nudged Captain's hand to get a head rub.

"Can't argue with that," I mumbled.

I caught up with the guys in the kitchen, where Roger was lifting the lids off pots and Forest was emerging from the cellar with a demijohn of home-brew. None of us are big drinkers, and Captain never makes his beer strong, but it's become tradition for us each to have a pint when we get together on Fridays. A nice way to unwind after a busy week. Busy for some of us, not so busy for the older generation.

Bellpepper, Dipple Sprocket, and Bingles dashed around the large, battered dining table picking up food scraps and aligning the cutlery perfectly as I watched from the doorway, smiling at the familiar sight of the Fairfield's doing what they do best. Getting together and not getting along. The gnomes refuse to stop until it's dark, so summer is always a hectic time for them, then they have the long winter months to recharge their batteries in the gardens. When they'd first arrived in the shop, I'd told them I didn't need any assistance, but they ignored me and got to work, "helping" keep the place in order and generally making my job twice as hard.

They mean well, and sometimes they are a real boon, but they have their own ideas about what neat and orderly means and will not be swayed.

"Hey Dad. Hey Uncle Frank." We bumped fists because we are men and that's what we do.

"Hi Bran," said Dad.

"Did you shut the shop?" asked Uncle Frank, Roger's dad.

"Of course. You don't need to ask me that every time. Why wouldn't I?"

"Just checking. Did you enjoy your oggie?"

"Had the food spies out, did you, Dad?" laughed Roger as he peeked into another saucepan.

"Watch your attitude," he warned, easing stray long grey hairs behind his large red ears. Our family seems to have a rule about hair. The older you get, the longer you wear it. The more grey, the more of a wizard you are. Even Captain has long hair, and annoyingly for Dad and Uncle Frank, it's thicker, more luscious, and curlier than theirs. He refuses to give up the potions used, and they've both spent the better part of two decades trying to deconstruct it to no avail.

"What's cooking?" I asked devilishly, bringing forth a groan from Roger and Forest.

Dad beamed, puffing out his chest as he took centre stage in the oversized kitchen. The first part of the renovations Dad insisted on was to knock down the wall between the old dining room and kitchen, even incorporating several other small rooms into one large space. It's the heart of the home now more than ever.

"Tonight, young fellows, we shall be feasting on slow roast leg of lamb marinated for twenty-seven hours precisely in my own top secret recipe. We have baby roast potatoes grown by Captain, beans lovingly nurtured by my own fair hands, butter supplied by..." On and on he droned while everybody looked anywhere but at him in the hopes that he'd stop talking. He didn't. Dad loves to cook—so does Uncle Frank, but not to the same degree. He's more the sidekick—and the only thing he loves more is to tell you about it.

To be fair, he's never made a bad meal in his life, apart from one time when the power went out halfway through a mammoth roast and the beef was ever-so-slightly tough, but we don't talk about that for fear of permanent banishment from the family home and being stripped of the name Fairfield. We also don't talk about Mum anymore, but that's another story.

"...So what do you think?" Dad spread his arms wide and beamed at us.

We exchanged a wry smile with Uncle Frank, then all blurted, "Sounds amazing."

Dad soaked up the praise and set about finishing up while we got everything together for dinner. I adjusted the cutlery after the gnomes had scampered off somewhere, Roger helped with plates, and Forest poured the beer.

Times like this are golden.

"Get ready, guys," warned Uncle Frank with a smirk.

We hurriedly took our places at the table, just so Captain couldn't whack us with his staff, and grinned as the oldest living Fairfield entered the kitchen with Kale by his side.

"What are you lot smirking at?" growled Captain.

"Just looking forward to dinner," I said, winking at Dad.

"I saw that!"

"No you didn't. You haven't got your glasses on."

"Still saw it," he grumbled, as he eased himself into the chair at the head of the table and gave his staff to Kale.

"Where'd you want it?" came the muffled voice of Kale, mouth full of wood.

"Same place as always."

Captain is the only other person that understands Kale, and they get on surprisingly well. Kale walked over to the other side of Captain then simply opened his mouth and let the staff fall to the floor. It rattled about for a while then finally was still. Captain grunted, everyone else shook their heads in wonder at the madness of such a routine. Job done, Kale sank into his bed beside the Aga and curled up.

"How was the show?" asked Roger.

"Great. There was this—"

"Who wants roasties?" asked Dad hurriedly.

Everyone did, duh, so Captain was drowned out while the meat, potatoes, veggies, and various salads were passed around.

"How was business today?" asked Uncle Frank, always keen to hear about the shop.

"Great actually. The heat doesn't seem to have stopped the tourists. I've got six orders for potions, and even the little guys were a help. Apart from Standin'," I whispered, checking he wasn't around, but you can never be sure.

"And I hear you have a date tomorrow," cackled Captain.

"How on earth did you know that, Grandad?" I asked, gobsmacked when I really shouldn't be.

But I'd made a fatal error, one I still can't get right every time, and the room fell silent as everyone stared at me, aghast.

"Here we go," groaned Roger.

"It's Captain," said, er, Captain. "Kale, pass me my staff."

Kale knew better than to dawdle, so snapped out of his snooze and passed the mighty lump of hallowed hazel to him then retreated. Captain banged it on the red quarry tiles then handed it back to Kale who dropped it, dashed to his bed, curled up, and put his massive paws over his ears.

"Traitor," I hissed.

Impression made, Captain began his usual rant. "The eldest in the family is always known as Captain. I will not be called Grandad in my own house."

"Technically—" began Dad, but that was as far as he got.

"The Fairfield's are deserving of the respect we have in this town, and we can't go around being called Grandad when we have history. Real history." He was warming up now, so really on a roll. "Your ancestor was a famous Captain of the sea and he bestowed the gift upon his ancestors to forever be known as Captain. I will not be spoken down to in such a manner." Captain lifted his fedora and ruffled his thick mane before replacing it. I think he even sleeps in it as I've never seen him without it for more than a few seconds. "We should all be proud of the sacrifices our ancestors made for us, and I will have my due respect."

"And you shall have it, Captain," I told him, not daring to even smirk.

"That's a good boy. You were always my favourite." Captain winked at me and his mouth twitched, but he scowled when the others turned to him and began bickering about how come I was the special one.

Captain ignored them all, undid a single button on his long johns—it's all he'll wear in the house, and when outside he keeps them on no matter the weather as he insists he feels the cold when we all know he doesn't as his magic is stronger than all of ours, maybe even combined—and began to eat his dinner with an evil glint in his eye.

Grandad has his version of events when it comes to the title of Captain, but Dad told us cousins a different version a few years ago.

Apparently our great-great-great-great-great grandfather had a boat. That was it. He had a boat. It sank. He then no longer had a boat. It wasn't even a big one. And it sank. End of story. But ever since, the eldest male Fairfield was known as Captain, and I still find it tough to remember, or maybe I just enjoy the banter. Prove it. I dare you.

I was aware of the room having turned several degrees cooler thanks to my innate wizard sense, or maybe it was because everyone was staring at me expectantly and my blood froze. Here we go.

"What?" I asked, dreading what I'd missed.

"I said," snapped Captain, "I hope you aren't going to blow it. She's a lovely girl and her gran was a dear friend. Even her mother's okay, I suppose," he added with a tug of his salt and pepper beard.

"Blow what?" I asked, hoping he was talking about something else, knowing he wasn't.

"Your date with Helen. That lovely girl who just moved back. Such a shame about her gran, and the poor girl's been single long enough. Perfect for you to swoop in," he cackled, the dirty old man.

"Who told?" I asked, glaring at Roger and Forest.

"Not me."

"Me neither."

"They didn't say a word, although they should have. Bad boys," he told them, wagging a twisted finger.

Both ducked, which was sensible. Sometimes Captain lets off too much steam. Literally. He boiled a can of sweetcorn once when I told him I didn't particularly like sage.

"Then who did?" I asked.

"Never you mind. You keep forgetting, I know this town and everyone in it. Nothing gets past Captain."

"Wow, talking in the third person now, are we?"

"What does that mean? Is it rude? Are you saying I'm a third of what I used to be? I'll have you know—"

"Dad," said Uncle Frank, "he's just saying you were referring to yourself as Captain."

"Well, I am," he huffed, folding his arms across his chest.

We agreed he was, which placated the mad long john wearing, finger-blasting wizard at the head of the table, and he grumbled something then continued like nothing had happened. "So, a date, eh?" he wiggled his bushy eyebrows like only a truly old wizard can.

"Kind of," I shrugged, acting cool and casual.

"You aren't fooling anyone," laughed Uncle Frank. "Helen's nice. I met her the other day. Her mum's sweet too."

"Don't you dare," I warned. He has a reputation around these parts. He "knows" more local women of a certain age than any other man I've ever met.

"What?" he asked, feigning innocence.

"Just don't."

"Where are you taking her? What are you doing? Have you got protection?" asked Captain.

"It's a first date. Not even a proper one!" I protested.
"I don't need protection."

"Every wizard needs his wards," Captain told me. I'm
sure he sniggered into his beard.

"Oh, right. Yes, all fine in that department, thanks.
And we're just going to have lunch. At least, I think that's
what we said." I couldn't for the life of me remember. Guess
I was more enamoured than I'd thought. "Oh, I was speaking
to Snodgrass earlier."

"That snake," spat Captain. He hates him with a
vengeance, always has.

"Yeah, he was moaning about Freddy again."

"Fat Freddy's a lovely young man," said Captain.

"You can't call him that!" said Dad.

"Why not? His name's Freddy and he's fat. He even
has it on his business card. I've got one somewhere."

"Really?" I asked.

"Yes. It says. Fat Freddy's Outdoors is Nice to Visit,
or something like that. He pays his rent on time. He's a good
person."

"Anyway, as I was saying. It got me thinking. How
come you didn't buy the other houses? You have the money,
you own lots of other property, but you never bought the
houses literally next door."

"Who says I didn't?"

I turned to the others; they shrugged.

"Captain," asked Dad, "are you saying you owned
them?"

"Course I did," he snapped. "Bought them years ago.
I was waiting."

"Waiting for what?" asked Forest.

"For you lot to get off your bums and do something
with them," he muttered.

"You owned them and let them fall into that state
just on the off chance we'd decide we wanted to renovate
them one day?" I asked, stunned.

"Yes, of course. It's obvious, isn't it?"

"Um, no."

"What about Dad and Uncle Frank? You didn't think they could have lived in them?"

"They couldn't get away from me quick enough," he chided. "I helped them both out, of course, but I knew their women wanted some distance. Fair enough. I am a handful, always have been."

"You can say that again," mumbled Uncle Frank.

"So you put them up for auction?" I asked. "Why?"

"Obvious. Are you all dumb? Bran was a mess, he lost his wife, but I knew he'd pull through, and when he did, I put them up for auction. I knew you'd come back. This is your home. The timing was right, as Forest had split from that horrid woman too, so I figured you'd want to be together."

"But what if we'd lost at the auction?" asked Roger.

"What if you had?" Captain shook his head then muttered under his breath before tucking into a roast potato like it had caused him grievous bodily harm in a past life.

The rest of us exchanged confused glances, but we shouldn't have been surprised. Captain rules our world, and always has, whether we know about it or not. He's been looking out for us our whole lives, just in his own twisted way.

Dinner continued in much the same vein. Everyone prying into everyone else's business, Captain grumbling, and us "youngsters" trying to just get through the evening before we were released.

We did the dishes and tidied up the kitchen while the old men relaxed in the living room, then went in to join them.

The news was on, and my head pounded as I watched, my heart sinking.

Trouble Brewing

"The poor man," I groaned, slumping onto the sofa when the news report was over. Uncle Frank turned off the TV so they could gossip like a bunch of decrepit hags.

"Hey, it happens," said Forest. "Every few years someone falls or jumps. It's a long drop, and some of those walkers need Zimmer frames. Not walking boots that cost more than a week's hard graft."

"Bitter much," I snapped. "Sorry, but that guy, he came into the shop with his wife today. I, er, I kinda told her to push him off. I tried to tell you earlier, but I didn't want Helen to hear about this."

Everyone stopped talking mid-sentence and turned to me.

"You what?" Captain leaned forward in his chair, eager for more information.

"Don't look so excited. And I was just joking. She was a nice elderly lady, and we were enjoying some banter. She asked if I could kill him for her. I told her to shove him off a cliff. That cliff."

"No way! Dude, that's awesome!" said Roger.

"It is not awesome. I didn't know what to do, so I called Calum."

"Why haven't I heard about this?" growled Captain.

"Because you prefer gossip about the neighbours, and our love life," said Roger.

"Do not," grumbled Captain.

"And we thought it best not to mention it over dinner," said Dad.

"You heard about this?" I asked.

"It happens sometimes," said Uncle Frank. "Silly sods get lost and take a tumble. But you called Calum? What happened?"

"I called." I turned to Roger and said, "It was not awesome."

Roger was suddenly serious. "Damn, sorry. Wasn't thinking. You guys spoken much since you came back? It's been years now."

"We spoke, and like I told you at the time, it went badly."

"I meant after that."

"No, not a word. He loathes me, blames me for his daughter's death, and I'm sick of the arguments. I assumed having to tell the police chief, your dead wife's father, who absolutely would rather I was dead and certainly not living here, that you told someone to commit murder would make his day. But he just dismissed it. The line was a bit crackly, but I think he heard everything. He said it was an accident. That his wife, Sheila, wasn't there."

"But you explained properly?" asked Dad, face full of sympathy.

"I tried. Yes, I'm sure I did. But you know Calum, and he wasn't happy to hear from me."

"Then you need to go and see him."

"Dad, what's the point? He said it was an accident."

"So your mind is at ease. If she asked about getting him murdered, even in jest, then Calum needs to know. Did you tell him that?"

"Um, no. We were just joking around. But I told him about me suggesting she push him. But maybe Calum wasn't paying attention, and the line was bad," I admitted.

"You are in for a world of hurt, my friend," agreed Forest with too much of a smirk.

"What are you laughing at?"

"Nothing. It's just funny."

"Forest, it really isn't. Things have been going well, I'm doing good at the shop, and this will ruin everything."

"No, it won't," said Dad, stepping in before Forest could say anything else stupid. "It might help build bridges. Now you guys have to talk to each other properly. And not on the phone. Maybe you can finally put the past behind you. He's not a bad man, but he hasn't handled this well. It's easy to judge, but he lost his daughter. I can't imagine how I'd feel."

"It's not that simple, is it? His daughter died in a car crash and I was driving. I live in his town. I'm a constant reminder. He hates me."

"You know it wasn't your fault." Dad came over and put his arm around me. I could smell his unmistakable scent of rosemary. He puts it in everything. Even sprinkles it on his Cornflakes.

"I know. It's the hardest thing I've ever had to come to terms with, but I know. But he won't accept it."

"Just go see him. Do it now, or you'll fester on it and it'll be ten times worse."

I nodded. He was right.

"Fancy a drive, guys?" I asked Forest and Roger hopefully.

"Sorry, but this one is on you. I'm not getting involved."

"Are you mad? He's one scary guy."

"Oh. Okay." I shrugged, disappointed, then got off the sofa.

"Of course we'll come, you numpty! You think I'd leave my brother to deal with this alone? We're a team, always have been, always will be. Roger's coming, right?" Forest turned to him and he nodded. "Great. You always know how to handle these kind of things."

"I do?" he asked, surprised.

"Of course."

"When has anything similar ever happened before?" I asked, nonplussed.

"We're always getting into scrapes together. Don't put yourself down. Ever since you came back, the town's a better place. People look up to you. They know you're smart and you've helped loads of them with problems. You figured out who trashed the leisure centre. You caught those sods who tipped over the ice-cream van. You found the missing donkey that those mad druggies nicked from the sanctuary. Loads of stuff. You're like Little Hope's own personal private eye. A wizardly one," he added, wiggling his eyebrows. He does it quite a lot now, practising for when he's a proper old wizard and has the bushiness.

"I don't think this is quite the same, and all those things you mentioned, Calum hates me for figuring them out. I heard he was baying for my blood. Making him look bad, is what he said."

"Screw him. You help this town, we all do. We're a team. Me and Roger the Lodger are part of it too. We look out for each other. Bros."

"Bros," I agreed.

"Will you guys stop calling me the lodger?" Roger stamped his foot. Our Dads and Captain stared at him. "What, now I'm the bad guy?"

"No foot stamping," Dad reminded him. "And I'm sure you lads will sort out this mess. Go easy on Calum, Bran. This could be the start of you sorting things out with him. Take a deep breath before you speak, and I mean every single time, and don't let him wind you up. Be cool. Like your dad."

"You lose your rag if someone says your potatoes are a little hard."

"My potatoes are not hard!" he shouted, then realised what he'd done and began to breathe in and out deeply. "He didn't mean it. He didn't mean it," he recited between breaths.

"Oh," said Captain, taking his staff from Kale and nodding his thanks, then standing, regaling us with a full frontal of him in all his grubby long john glory. "Don't forget you need to find out who killed Helen's gran." He sank back into his chair and handed his staff back to Kale who just let it go.

"What! You never mentioned that," we screamed.

"I'm sure I did," he said, then frowned and stroked his beard. Bits of potato dropped to the floor that Kale devoured greedily.

"Kale, that's gross."

"I'm a dog. Deal with it," he mumbled, snorting up rug fluff in his eagerness to get the meagre offerings.

"Dad, what are you talking about? She died quite a while ago and there was no mention of foul play. She was old. She died. That was it."

"Was it?" he asked, growling as he gave Uncle Frank the evil Captain stare.

"Um, yes. And you never mentioned this before. What's going on?"

"Come on, Captain," said Roger eagerly, sitting in front of the old man with his legs crossed, craning forward like he was about to have a bedtime story for a man fast-approaching forty.

We crowded around him; Captain's chest swelled with the attention. He loves this kind of stuff.

"Ready?" he asked, looking at each of us in turn.

We nodded eagerly, which was when I became aware that we were all rather too keen on this juicy bit of horrific gossip.

"Ha, gotcha!" he cackled, then had a coughing fit and his eyes watered as he laughed and choked and spluttered.

"Not funny," I said.

"So stupid," muttered Dad.

"Very childish," snapped Uncle Frank.

"Captain, that was evil," Roger warned.

Captain wiped his eyes with a grubby sleeve and told us, "You should have seen your faces. You couldn't wait for the gossip. Right bunch of busybodies, all of you."

"Us?" I asked, gobsmacked. "And you shouldn't make fun of the dead."

"Oh, she doesn't mind, do you?" he asked, turning to his right and speaking to the air.

"She isn't here, is she?" asked Roger in a panic.

"Gotcha again!" the mad old git chuckled. "There are no ghosts in this house. At least, not today," he added sinisterly. This time he wasn't joking. We've had our fair share over the years.

"I need to go see Calum," I told everyone.

"You want me to come?" asked Dad.

"Best not to. You aren't his favourite person either. See you tomorrow."

"Good luck."

"I'm gonna need it."

We said our goodbyes then the four of us piled out, went back to our house to let Kale in, then jumped in my beat-up old Land Rover. The guys had laughed when I'd bought it as they had more modern pickups they used for work, but I'd always wanted one so did exactly that.

It was pushing nine by now, so Calum Swift would be at home. I wasn't sure if that was a good thing or not. At least if we were at the small police station, there would be witnesses if anything went awry. I told myself there was nothing to be ashamed of, that I'd done nothing wrong, but sometimes your mind simply won't give you the peace you know you deserve.

My wife, Emily, may not be a ghost, but she'll haunt me 'til my dying day.

Deep Breath

There are no lights outside the centre of town. Even on Wizard's Way there are only a few. We prefer to keep it dark and mysterious for obvious reasons.

I navigated the pitch black lanes like only someone born and bred in Little Hope could do. Within minutes, we were parked outside the turn to Calum Swift's cottage.

"I haven't been here for years," I sighed, distant memories returning, some of which I'd rather forget. "He wouldn't let me past the gate the last time I came. I just wanted to talk about Emily, you know."

"We know," said Forest. "You tried. That was all you could do. He was hurting, still is. We have to remember that."

"He's a good guy," added Roger. "We had some fun times here over the years."

"We used to have parties. Emily was always so happy here. Whenever we came back, we'd all get together, even Captain, and have great nights barbecuing. Remember?"

"We remember," said Forest. "She was a great woman, Bran. We miss her too."

"I know you do. Look, I think I better go alone. I don't want him to think we're trying to bully our way in or anything. And you know he's going to say something stupid and I don't want you guys getting riled up. Okay?"

"Sure, whatever you want," said Forest.

Roger nodded.

"I'm sorry about this. You both usually go off to see your partners after dinner, and I've messed it up. Did you call and explain to them?"

"We called. It's cool. Family comes first at times like this," said Forest.

With a deep breath, I got out of the car and opened the gate. I closed it quietly behind me, pausing to look at the small cottage Emily had grown up in. Memories came flooding back. Of Christmas and birthdays and visits and me nervously knocking on the door before our first date. So long ago now. I was another person. Little more than a boy. But I'd known she was the one ever since we were teenagers, and when I finally got up the nerve to ask her out at sixteen, I felt like all my Christmases had come at once when she said yes.

We'd been together ever since. We grew into adults together. We shared our lives, everything. Set up our first home, moved away for the first time. We were a team. Inseparable. And then she was gone. Dead.

My whole world fell apart.

Calum Swift, local Police Chief, and once a very jovial man, was understandably distraught. We spoke on the phone, but once he was told what had happened he refused to speak to me again. I tried over and over, even came back to see him, but he just shouted and cried and blamed me until I couldn't take it any longer. We hadn't spoken in three years since I tried one more time when I returned.

When we passed on the street he blanked me. He was friendly enough to the rest of the family in an aloof way, but when it came to me I was as dead as his daughter to him. I didn't blame him. How could I?

Didn't mean I agreed with him. I'd gone through the usual emotional turmoil, blaming myself, ranting, raving, all of it. Then, finally, I understood it wasn't my fault. Just one of the things that happens, even to the nice people in the world. I knew it wasn't my fault. Deep down, I think Calum did, too. He just wasn't ready to let go of blame just yet. Maybe one day. I hoped so, more for his sake than mine. You can't live your life feeling nothing but bitterness. Eventually, you have to accept that life isn't always fair and try your best to enjoy the beauty our world has to offer.

Calum loves his town, and has never wanted to rise above the role of Police Chief as becoming an Inspector or Chief Inspector would mean he'd have to relocate to a main branch out of Little Hope. He used to be happy running the small team of three that looked after the wider area, and there were hardly any times that he had to call in the big guns as crimes here are petty, easily solved, or something he and his team could easily deal with. Now he just goes through the motions.

Luckily, being surrounded by the likes of us means he always has help when it's needed. Calum may not be a blessed individual in magical matters, but he is a gifted, competent policeman who likes a quiet life, loves his hometown, and adored his family. Now he is alone.

The security lights lit up the yew trees as I crossed the gravel drive. Before I had chance to get to the small green door, it was opened by Calum. He still wore his uniform; guess he'd had a late finish. Fridays are usually busier when people let their hair down and the freaks crawl out of the woodwork. Nothing major, but being a slightly unusual town, there is always a small fire or an over-excited witch to deal with. Calum had always taken it in his stride. He'd been married to a witch, accepted magic was real, and never judged. Until me.

"What do you want, Bran?" he asked with a weary sigh. "We have nothing more to say to each other. I already told you that. Leave me alone. Are you drunk, is that it? I hope you didn't drive."

"I'm not drunk. I had a beer with dinner, that's all."

"Oh, yes, Family Dinner Friday. How nice," he sneered, then caught himself and was about to apologise, but shook his head and just said, "Go home." He moved back into the house and went to close the door, but I stepped forward.

"It's about the death, Calum. I have information."

"We already spoke. You said your piece. It's under control. One of those things."

"I hope you're right, but I still need to talk to you. Can I come in?"

"Absolutely not. Say what you have to say, then leave me be. I've had a long week, and I have the weekend off, for once, so get on with it."

"The man's wife, she, er..." How did I put this? "Let me start again. Sheila and her husband came into the shop earlier. He waited outside after a while, and she was complaining about how he was grumpy. She asked me, joking, of course, if I could kill him for her. Just banter. I don't think I told you that part."

"No, but it doesn't matter."

"It doesn't?" I asked, surprised.

"No, now please go home."

"Let me finish. Just so I know I've done the right thing. I, er, I said maybe she should just shove him off the quarry. Maybe not in those words, but I mimed a shove, and she knew what I meant. Sorry, this is coming out all wrong. It's probably nothing, but I felt I had to tell you in person. The line was crackly and I need to know you understand me properly. Just in case. She seemed nice, really friendly, and she's coming in for a reading tomorrow. At least she was. I wasn't sure what to do, so figured it was best to come and see you."

Calum stared at me for a long time, face blank, his trim white beard and short hair making him appear every ounce the practised policeman. "You finished?"

"I guess," I shrugged.

"Let me get this straight. You had some banter with a woman complaining about her husband being a grouch, she asked jokingly if you'd kill him, you said no, but maybe she could shove him off the quarry, and you thought I should know? Is that correct?"

"That's about it." It was beginning to sound lame, even to me. She wouldn't do that, would she? I didn't think so, but I had to pass on the information just in case.

Calum sighed. "Go home. Just go away. Why are you still doing this to me, Bran?"

"Doing what? I thought you should know."

"It's an excuse. We already spoke. What, you think we can be best friends? You killed my daughter. You killed her." Calum wiped his eyes; he was hurting so bad.

"It was an accident. I swear. I loved her."

"You killed my little girl. That vehicle of yours was a death trap. I had it checked over. The brakes were shot, the lines were so threadbare they'd go at any moment. You should have known better. You were speeding. The speedo was jammed, so I know you were going too fast."

"No, that's not right," I stammered, confused. "It had just passed the MOT. The service was done too. It was in great condition. And I wasn't speeding. We were nearly here. I know the lanes like the back of my hand. The brakes gave out, but I swear it had been fine up until then."

"Just go away."

"What about the death?"

"Just this once, I'll talk, but don't bother me again. The 'guy' as you put it, was a seasoned hiker. He went walking alone while his wife was having her aura read by young Macy. She was nowhere near him when he died. I told you that. You shouldn't have come here. It was an unfortunate accident, Bran, nothing more. You happy now? Because I'm just ecstatic. Peachy, in fact."

"That's good, that's great. I mean, she didn't do it. Look, Calum, if you just..."

He slammed the door.

I walked back to the car in a daze.

"How did it go?" asked Forest from the passenger seat.

"You okay?" asked Roger, putting a hand on my shoulder.

"Let's just go home, then I'll tell you. But he definitely wasn't murdered, so that's good."

The guys murmured their agreement, but they sensed my mood. We drove home in silence.

"Thanks." I took the coffee from Roger with a weak smile and sipped the sweet drink. It was too hot, so I put it on the table and ruffled Kale's head. He hadn't left my side since we returned.

"What happened?" asked Kale.

"It was weird, that's what. I don't want to say this twice, so I'll tell you all at the same time."

"Do I need to bite anyone?" said Kale, trying to lighten the mood.

"No. Not yet anyway."

The guys sat on the sofa, waiting for me to speak. I wasn't even sure what to say, if there was anything that needed saying. But maybe they'd be able to help figure this out. Was this a thing, or just a distraught father clutching at straws?

I sighed, then began to talk. "First of all, Calum said that Sheila, the dead guy's wife, was having her aura read when he died. He was walking alone. So she didn't push him. Calum did say that on the phone, but now we know she was nowhere near him."

"That's good, right?" said Roger, nodding.

"Yeah."

"But there's something else, isn't there?" asked Kale.

"Kale asked if there was something else," I told the others. "There is."

"Spill it then," said Forest, never the most patient.

"Calum said that the car was a wreck."

"You crashed, it was a write-off," said Roger softly. "We all saw it. You were lucky to get out alive."

"No, not that. He said he had the car checked over. Reckoned the brakes were worn down, and the lines, you know, that carry the brake fluid, were threadbare. Said it was neglect. And that's not all. He said the speedo was jammed after the crash and I'd been speeding."

"You never speed," said Forest.

"You're a right wuss behind the wheel. You always go slow. It's really lame," said Roger.

"I know, right? But I've always been wary of cars. It's nuts that you have this massive lump of metal that can go wrong at any time. You know I've always been neurotic about getting my cars checked out. New tyres, new brakes, everything. I always follow the service schedule and I never speed. I don't even overtake." I rubbed at my face. This was all just weird.

"So he reckons you were speeding and the car wasn't fit to drive?" asked Forest.

"That's what he said. It doesn't make sense. It hadn't long passed its MOT, the service was done just before that, and it drove like a dream."

"Then he's wrong. The speedo could easily have got stuck at any speed. It was mangled. Doesn't mean you were driving at that speed." Forest nodded to Roger. "Right?"

"Of course. He's just upset, clutching at straws."

"This is why he blames me. He always said it was my fault, and now we know why. But what about the brakes?"

"Bran, you're a nice guy, but you have to admit you know nothing about cars. And I bet Calum doesn't either. He hasn't got the time to go fiddling about with them. He's as clueless as you are. You've seen what he drives. It's a Vauxhall Cavalier from the Flintstones!"

"But he said the lines were all trashed. Frayed, he said."

"You don't get frayed brake lines," said Roger. "They're rubber tubes, sometimes metal. They can split, sure, and you get leaking brake fluid, or they can be cut, but they don't fray. That doesn't happen."

"You sure?"

"I'm sure," he nodded. "And the brakes will have worn badly when you crashed. They locked up as you broke so hard. Then you skidded down the lane for ages. The rubber marks were there for years. It was one hell of a slide. That will have trashed the brakes."

"He's right," agreed Forest. "I don't know as much as Roger, but that makes more sense than... Well, what?"

"I don't know. He basically accused me of letting the car get into a bad state and then speeding so I lost control and killed Emily. You sure about the brake lines and the speedo?"

"Positive. Calum's sad, and he's been depressed for years. Guess he's been stewing on this since the accident and built it up in his head until he convinced himself it's proof of your guilt. We know better. We know you. You don't speed. Ever. You look after your cars. You spend way too much on tyres and brake pads when we always tell you it's a waste of money and you should do what everyone else does. Wait for the garage to tell you when they need replacing. Brakes and lines don't suddenly wear out unless something drastic happens. It's simply not how cars work. So don't go reading anything into this."

"Like what?" They exchanged a worried look. "Like what?" I repeated.

"Like maybe someone is messing with you? Maybe someone tampered with the car before or after the crash to make it appear as though it was your fault or to cause the accident in the first place. Because it was just that. An accident. I don't know what Calum thinks he saw, but he's wrong. You got the insurance payout. The car was checked after the crash. You think the insurance inspector wouldn't have wanted to find signs of negligence? Course he would. Then they have an excuse not to pay. The car was clean. He will have gone over it with a fine-tooth comb. Plus the police at the time. Calum's no expert on crash investigation."

"Could someone have? Tampered with it, I mean? Caused the crash? And the inspector didn't find what Calum did?"

"No," said Roger. "If you cut brake lines then the brakes just won't work. You'd know straight away. And the speedo was working, right?"

"Of course it was!"

"He checked out the car, saw the damage from the crash, and read what he wanted to into it. End of," said Forest. "But he's no expert. The real experts gave it the all clear. Said it was because they hadn't put up the signs for roadworks and the simple fact is you drove straight into a bloody JCB just there on the road."

"End of," agreed Roger.

"Thanks guys. What a mess. I feel sorry for him. All these years, he's had this in his head. That I was negligent. No wonder he blames me."

"He needs someone to blame," said Roger. "He lost his daughter. Who could accept that? You want it to be someone's fault, not just one of those things that happens."

"One of those things that happens," I whispered.

"You know I didn't mean it like that," said Roger, looking flustered.

"No, you're right," I told him. "It's what I've finally come to terms with. It was just one of those things."

"I'm so sorry," said Kale, resting his head on my lap. "You just wanted to do the right thing and tell him about Sheila. That was good. He's just confused and angry."

"I know. But to have that resentment and anger all this time, it's madness."

We drank our coffee in silence, but it was doing no good. To cheer us up, and put this sorry night behind us, we watched Ghostbusters. The original, of course. It's Kale's favourite too. He loves the Terror Dogs, the demonic hellhounds. Says he wants to be just like them one day.

But I couldn't help wondering. Had the car been checked over by the insurance company? The firm digging the road didn't have a leg to stand on. They admitted liability, and it was obvious why we'd crashed. How thorough was the investigation? I'd never thought about it, was in a daze through the whole process. Stupid, but this is where your mind goes when you dwell on the past. Nowhere good.

I had to put it out of my head. I'd driven myself mad over the years running through different scenarios. It was done. Calum could believe what he wanted. I knew the truth. It was an accident.

Snitch!

"Hey Mum," I said as I flicked on the lights to Bran's Dream and turned the sign on the door to OPEN.

As usual, there was no reply.

Last night had left me utterly out of sorts. I could tell myself a million times that this was in the past, but Calum made it so hard. When would he forgive me? And why did I need his forgiveness anyway? We'd always got along well enough, but it wasn't like we were close.

Truth is, I didn't like to think of him hurting. And now I knew why he blamed me, it was even worse. He'd gone all these years believing I put his daughter's life at risk either on purpose or because I was so blasé about her safety that I plain didn't care. Surely he knew me better than that?

But what could I do? He wouldn't listen to reason, and he wasn't about to change his opinion.

"I could really do with a cuddle about now," I told the curled-up hedgehog on the bench in my cubby. The hedgehog unfurled itself and snuffled about, tiny eyes searching, nose twitching rhythmically.

"Did you actually understand that?" I mused. Sometimes Mum acts like she understands, other times she makes no sign she's anything but a hedgehog. I decided to believe what I wanted to believe, same as we all do, same as Calum, and carefully cradled Mum in my arms. I sat on my stool and told her what had happened, surprised to find I was crying. Not even for my loss, but for Calum. He's a hard man, but nobody deserves to go through what he has.

When I was done, I kissed Mum very carefully on her little pink nose, placed her back on the bed, wiped my eyes, and put out her favourite. Cat food. She eagerly tucked into it while I got about the business of the day. I missed my mum so much. Her and Dad's relationship was often complicated, but the one thing she has always been is a great mum. Until I came home. Then she did this to herself.

A new day, another chance to make it the best one yet. My spirits lifted when I thought about Helen. She'd be around at lunchtime, and I couldn't wait to see her. Life was good. Life was great. Life was about to get even better.

Guess Sheila wouldn't be showing up today. Certainly if she got wind of me going to see the local Police Chief. Although that was probably the last thing she had to worry about. Calum made it clear she wasn't involved. That it was just an accident. She was a sweet woman and I was glad she had no involvement. Did this make me a snitch? Running off to the law to tell on an old woman who was undoubtedly grieving? Who was I kidding? I'd be a mess of stress if I hadn't told Calum what had happened. People of every age kill each other all the time. Just because you're old doesn't mean you don't have hate in your heart. It just means you do your killing slower, and your joints will hurt more after. You'll probably need a nap too.

Saturday morning was the usual mix of utter boredom followed by too many customers at once, a manic tidy-up between the onslaught of families with kids running wild and picking up almost everything in the shop then putting it down somewhere random, and me trying to corral the gnomes to help rather than hinder.

It was just how I liked it. Perfect. The till kept ringing, the card reader kept beeping, and the customers kept on spending. I told the story about my shop name fifty times, I joked about gnomes a hundred, I laughed at the children poking Bignoodle where no gnome likes to be poked, and before I knew it the clock struck twelve and bonged—yes, I have a big clock that literally says, "Bong," but don't ask, it's a long story—so it was time for lunch.

What should I do? Should I just wait until half-past when Helen said she would arrive? Or did I go out and grab something for both of us and bring it back here? What if she didn't like it? What if she was early? What if she was late? What if she didn't come at all?

What on earth was wrong with me? I was acting like a desperate teen. I reminded myself again that I was a man in his thirties and had been on plenty of dates before, several had even been relationships for a while, and there was nothing to stress about. Sure, she was nice, but I wasn't a bad catch either. I have great hair, keep myself in shape, can even be funny, and I am always told I have nice eyes and am easy to talk to. She was lucky to be going on a date with me and was probably more nervous than I was.

I chuckled to myself. Yeah, right. I was definitely the lucky one. She was gorgeous, funny, had a nice aura, and an even nicer bum.

What had I planned for this afternoon? What would she expect? An oggie? Um, probably not. A sandwich? Picnic in the park? A walk in the woods? A drink at the local? I began to panic. I hadn't planned anything at all. How long was this meant to last? Were we meant to have an afternoon together or just an hour or so? Why hadn't I made a lovely picnic and organised a hamper? That would have made a good impression. Instead, I was here in my Levi's, a faded blue t-shirt, and I hadn't even washed my hair this morning. It always looks wrong for a day or two until it recovers from a good scrubbing.

The bell above the door clanged, snapping me out of my reverie. I really was stressed. I hadn't even locked up.

"Sheila? What are you doing here?"

"I've come for my Tarot reading," she said, looking confused as she let the door go and the bell bounced about. I needed to get rid of it. The thing was becoming beyond annoying. Why bother? I was always here.

"But what about your husband?"

"He's dead," she sighed, brushing her hand through her stiff grey curls. Her make-up was immaculate, she was dressed for hiking, and her hands were steady. How was she taking this so well?

"I know. I heard yesterday on the news. I'm so sorry. Here, come and take a seat in the cubby. It's cramped, but you can take the weight off."

"Are you saying I'm fat?" she chuckled.

"No, there's nothing of you. Nothing a few oggies wouldn't cure."

"I had one yesterday, but couldn't finish it. Very nice though."

"I'll have to give you the recipe. Um, no, I don't know it."

Sheila smiled halfheartedly and sank onto the stool. I perched myself on the bench, careful not to get a bum full of hedgehog spines.

"Sheila, seriously, what are you doing here? Your husband died. It's terrible. How are you handling it?"

"I'm okay. No, I'm not. Daft old bugger might have been a pain, but that's no way to go. Especially not for him. And I understand you paid a visit to the local police last night?"

"How did you hear about that?"

"He came to see me this morning at the campsite. Said he just wanted to confirm the conversation. He was rather pushy, and I think he'd been drinking. His breath smelled sour. I got the impression he's not a fan of yours. He was angling for me to say something bad about you. I think he wanted me to say I suspected you or something."

"Sorry about that. After our conversation yesterday, and what you said, well, I knew you had nothing to do with it, but I wanted to let Calum know. Just doing the right thing, you understand?"

"Of course I do. I would have done the same. It's best to be upfront. It was just a joke. You mimed pushing him off a cliff. We laughed about it. That was it. And yes, I know I asked if you could kill him. But it was a joke. You do believe me, don't you?"

"Of course I do. Like I said, I just wanted to do the right thing. What did Calum say?"

Sheila shrugged. "Same as he did yesterday when he came to tell me what happened. It looked like he slipped and fell. That's it." Sheila gnawed on her bottom lip, her hands gripped her small bag tight.

"Anything else?"

"He gave me some numbers to call. Albert's with the coroner, but I will need to organise getting him sent back home. But I can't."

"Why not?"

"Because," she looked up and met my eyes, face set firmly in determination, "there is absolutely no way he fell off a bloody cliff, excuse my French. And I hear you're the man to find out what happened. I told the police the same, but they didn't seem to care. Oh, they said they'll look into it, but I could tell they would just go through the motions. Will you help me? Please?"

"Why don't you think he fell? Hikers are always having accidents. Falling off mountains, slipping, getting rescued. Or not," I added lamely.

"I know all that, but not Albert. You met him, you saw how he was. He was a grump, but I loved him."

"Of course you did," I agreed, handing over a tissue.

She dabbed at her eyes then said, "He was a cautious man. Very risk averse. We do, did, a lot of hiking. We always had the very best gear. He insisted. We always, always took emergency equipment. Flares, packs of food, matches in those waterproof containers, water, those foil blankets. All of it. I always told him I just wanted to go on a walk, not feel like a mule, but he insisted."

"I'm not sure what you're getting at."

"I'm telling you that he was a cautious, responsible man. I've been on hundreds, no, thousands of walks and hikes with that man and he had one rule."

"Go on."

"Don't stand anywhere near the edge."

"He could have slipped."

"The police said he must have slipped too, but I don't believe it. He wouldn't have stood near the edge. If he fell over, he wouldn't have fallen off a cliff. Albert was cautious. It drove me crazy. He did not fall. He might be a little forgetful at times, always misplacing his keys, which, by the way, the police didn't find so I had to use the spare, but he took safety seriously. "

"He might have seen something and got too close," I offered.

"Like what?"

"A bird. An animal. Who knows? Maybe he thought he heard something and went to take a look. Maybe he stumbled and couldn't stop. Sheila, it could have been anything. What are you suggesting happened?"

"Someone pushed him. They must have."

"And did he have enemies? Why would anyone do that?"

"He had a lot of people that didn't exactly like him. But that's back home. We're tourists. We've only been here since yesterday. We parked at the campsite early yesterday morning and by lunchtime he was dead. We don't know anyone here."

"There you go then. You're strangers here. You just arrived. So there's no reason anyone would push him. He was probably tired, might have had a dizzy spell. Maybe he got disorientated, felt dizzy, stumbled, and wham!" I banged my fist on the table, making Sheila jump and Mum whimper. "Sorry, didn't mean to do that." What an idiot.

Sheila's cheeks flushed with the shock of my banging, but she held my gaze and told me, "He did not slip."

"Was he on any medication? Did he have diabetes? Could his blood sugar levels have crashed? Maybe that made him disorientated."

"Yes, he took insulin. The policeman, Calum Swift, was it?" I nodded. "He said they'd do an autopsy and that will most likely be the cause. He probably took a funny turn and slipped."

"There you go then. Calum's a good guy, and I'm sure he's right."

"That man did not slip. I'm telling you he was very cautious. He took his meds yesterday morning. I saw him. They were low dose and he hardly needed them. He was fine. He was pushed."

"You're very sure of this, aren't you?"

"Positive."

I nodded, then said, "Okay, there's one way to be sure. You still want your reading?"

"It's why I'm here. To prove to you this was a murder, and I want you to help me."

"I promise I will, if the cards say you're right."

"They will." She nodded eagerly, clearly convinced. Grief can do funny things to a person. The best thing to do was let the cards tell us what really happened. Then she could grieve properly, knowing this was a terrible accident.

We exited the cubby and I was about to lead her to the back room where I conduct the other side of my business when the bell jangled again. "I'm definitely getting rid of it," I muttered before turning. I'd still forgotten to lock up, too.

Standing there, grinning, were Forest and Roger.

"What are you guys doing here? I thought you had a busy day?"

"We do, but we thought we'd come to check you were ready for your big date," said Roger, grinning like the idiot he undoubtedly is.

"Oh no, what time is it?"

"Ten past," laughed Forest. "Look at you. Bit stressed, aren't you?" He nudged Roger and told him, "He's a wreck."

"I'm fine. It's just a date," I shrugged.

"Liar," laughed Roger. "Look at your hair. It's all over the place. And I bet you haven't even done a hamper. Good job we know how useless you are at getting organised."

"I'm organised. And look, I don't have time for this. Sheila needs my help. Sheila, this is my brother, Forest, and our cousin, Roger."

Sheila smiled weakly and they both turned serious.

"So sorry about your loss."

"You have our deepest sympathy."

"Thank you both. I've been telling Bran that it was no accident. My Albert was pushed, and Bran's about to prove it."

Forest and Roger looked to me for an explanation, so I told them, "I'm going to do a reading. Sheila's a believer, so this will tell us the truth. Then she can grieve."

"I'll grieve when we catch the killer," she said, squaring her shoulders.

I caught the wave of excitement passing through my brother and cousin. They love this kind of thing. Our family is always involved in one mystery or another, or meddling where we shouldn't, especially the older generation, but Forest and Roger, and yes me too, love the chance to get involved in the magical side of our community. This was different, though. This was a death. A grieving widow. We had to tread carefully.

"I'll see you guys later, okay?"

"Can't they help?" asked Sheila.

"Yes, we can," said Roger eagerly. "I've got a hamper for you outside. I'll set things up ready so that when Helen arrives you're good to go."

"A hamper? Seriously?"

"We know what you're like. You'll try to make a mess of this without knowing that's what you're doing. You always sabotage your dates."

"I do not. Why would I?"

"Because you don't think you deserve to be happy. You do. And we're going to make sure you don't mess up."

"Plus, we want the work," laughed Forest.

"Yeah, that too," said Roger with a wry smile.

"Are you all wizards?" asked Sheila.

"What do you think?" I asked cautiously.

"I've heard a lot about you all, and I researched before we came. They say half the town are witches, wizards, or supernatural. And I'm sure that baker is a giant. He shimmered yesterday, and I saw him hunched over. A true giant."

"You must have some of the gift in you to see that. Yes, we are wizards. Most don't believe, but it's true. Not pretend, but the real deal."

"I knew it. That's why I want you to find the killer. You lovely boys too," Sheila said, turning to them. "The more the merrier. Hmm, maybe that's the wrong phrase. Will you help me?"

"I'll bring the hamper in, then we'll come into the back room," said Roger. "We'll get a better reading if all three of us are present. It increases the energy."

I shook my head in despair, but he was right. Combined, our power is much greater.

"Fine," I conceded. "But get a move on. Sorry about this, Sheila, I was just expecting to go on my date. I assumed you wouldn't show up."

"Oh, it's fine. Is she nice? A lovely lad like you, I bet you can have your pick of the girls."

"Yes, she's very nice. And I haven't been called a lad in some time."

"When you get to my age, dear, anyone under sixty is a youngster. Lead the way." Sheila grabbed my arm so I showed her the back room. I glanced over my shoulder at the others. They were grinning ear to ear. They were loving this.

"Kale, you coming?"

"Of course. It wouldn't be much of a reading without me, would it?"

The Cards Never Lie

The back room is everything non-believers, and believers alike, expect. Low level red lighting, lots of skulls, several stuffed birds I've picked up from antique markets or that were gifted by wizards, bunches of herbs, numerous vials and bottles of potions, and I even have a crystal ball. It's faulty though, as all I can get is BBC2.

The small round table is covered in a black cloth, not a crease on it. The cards are always there waiting in a neat stack.

Sheila took the seat I indicated while I settled myself opposite after lighting an incense stick and several thick candles that are now stuck fast to an old sideboard. Kale sat beside me, head resting on the table, watching Sheila intently.

I reached out and indicated for Sheila to place her hands palm up on the table. I placed mine on hers. With her full focus on me, I asked, "Are you ready for this? You might not get the answers you want, or expect. But the cards always tell the truth. Do you trust me, Sheila?"

"I trust you, and I'm ready."

She was speaking the truth. Most people don't believe in Tarot, viewing it as little more than a parlour trick, a way to be told a load of nonsense by someone who looks the part, but it doesn't stop them wanting a reading. Same with seances. Not that I offer such a service. The dead are enough trouble without them hanging around the shop.

Kale and I locked eyes before settling into a place where we almost become the same being. As much dog as human, as much human as dog. I suddenly fancied sniffing Sheila's bum, so I knew I was in the right kind of zone. Settled, and ensconced in our magic, we began.

I shuffled the cards, let our energy seep once more into the deck like it had for over a hundred years as they were passed down the generations. Then I dealt, spreading them out in a semicircle on the cloth. A five-card spread.

Kale leaned forward and nudged a card with his nose.

Sheila's eyes darted from Kale to me, and I nodded. "Yes, Kale does the reading. Or I do. Or we both do. It's complicated." Bless her heart, she didn't bat an eyelid, merely nodded and watched Kale intently as he finished picking the order the cards were to be revealed. The card choice is just as important as the reading of the symbols; a truly symbiotic relationship.

"Every practitioner has a different way of reading the cards, but the Fairfields do things their own way. We have our system perfected, and it's never wrong. Do you understand what I'm telling you, Sheila?" I had to be sure.

"I understand. I'll accept your, and Kale's, reading. I trust you. I don't know why, but I do."

"The images will be unconventional," I explained. "They were drawn by an ancestor, so don't be shocked. But they are always right. You can change your mind. I'm not charging either way, so please speak now."

"I don't want to change my mind. But I'll pay you. I always pay my way." Sheila played with the fringe of her lightweight scarf, clearly nervous now we were on the verge of revelation.

"Okay then." I picked up my staff from beside me, although it wasn't strictly necessary, but the showman in me couldn't help it. Slowly, I hovered the thick, knobbly end of the unwieldy wood over each card in turn from left to right. When I'd finished, I settled my staff across the table beneath the cards and told Sheila, "Watch."

One by one, in their destined order, the cards turned over. As they did, so I moved the first to the left and each subsequent one to the right of the previous until the last card was revealed.

"It's real magic," gasped Sheila, who had done well to remain silent so long.

"It is," I agreed. "Shall we read the cards together?"

"Yes."

Our eyes lowered to the cards. It was exactly what I'd feared.

I explained to Sheila how the order of the cards was important. How each subsequent card helped interpret the previous, but that in this case little was needed beyond the obvious.

There was no doubt about it. Her husband, Albert, had most definitely been murdered, and she was next.

"Me? But why? And why Albert?"

"I guess that's what we'll have to find out."

Relief washed over her as she finally broke into a flood of tears. Kale barked, which didn't help, and as I stood to offer comfort, the door flew open and in rushed Helen.

"Hi," I said, smiling lamely at her. "I don't always bring women into the back room and make them cry, but it does happen more often than I'd like," I joked.

Helen looked bewildered, Sheila laughed so hard she had a coughing fit, Kale bounded over and nudged Helen's hand until she began stroking his head absentmindedly, and I gave my silent thanks to the cards before shuffling them, cleansing them of the reading, and putting them neatly back in their case. I glared at the guys until they squirmed. They shrugged and had the decency to look sorry about letting Helen barge in without explaining what was happening.

Sheila wiped her eyes and asked, "What now? Can we go and get the murderer?"

"What murderer?" asked a worried looking Helen.

"Guess this isn't the date you were expecting," I said.

"Actually," she said, dimples pulling me towards her like I was tethered, "I suspected it wouldn't be anything conventional. Um, is that incense? Oh no."

"It's only sandalwood. Nothing weird."

"No, I have to get out of here!" But it was too late. Before she had chance to even turn, she sneezed.

"That pretty girl's turned into a rabbit!" shrieked Sheila, stating the very obvious.

"Shall I get some lettuce?" grinned Forest.

"No, they prefer carrots," said Roger.

"Guys, enough with the jokes. Sheila, are you okay?"

"She's a rabbit." Sheila bent and picked Helen up then stroked her back. Helen's whiskers twitched as she nibbled on Sheila's sleeve.

"I'm not sure you should pick her up," I warned.

"Whyever not?"

"If she sneezes again, she'll be very heavy. Um, not that I'm saying you're fat," I told the Helen bunny. "You're just right. Nice and curvy in all the right places. And your bum is..." everyone was staring at me. "I'll keep quiet now."

"Good idea," said Forest, shaking his head.

"It's been a long morning," I offered by way of explanation.

"Nobody's that dumb, are they?" asked Roger. "He even managed to insult her when she's a rabbit. How is that even possible?"

"I can insult anyone at any time!" I shouted. Again with the looks. "You know what I mean."

"We really don't," said Roger.

Sheila and Forest shook their heads.

"Okay, can we please calm down? Helen, please sneeze." We waited, but she remained a rabbit.

"We need to go where he fell," said Sheila. "Maybe you can use your skills to look into the past? Can you do that? Will we be able to see what happened? Down where he hit, we can see from there. See who it was."

I exchanged a look with the guys. They nodded. We could do this. We had plenty of time before reading the scene would be nigh on impossible, but the sooner we did this the clearer the image would be.

"We can do that," I told her. "Are you up to it?"

"Yes, but I need a pee first."

"Me too," I realised.

"And me," said Roger. "I had three coffees this morning, so I definitely need a wee."

We turned to Helen rabbit. She weed on Sheila's lap.

"At least one of us doesn't need to go any more," I joked.

"It's fine," said Sheila. "I was a nurse for a long time, so bunny wee is nothing. I've been covered head-to-toe in much worse."

Helen sneezed as Sheila dabbed at her leg with a tissue, taking it in her stride. Next thing we knew, Helen was sitting in Sheila's lap.

"Did I just pee on you? Oh, I am so sorry. I'm mortified. And now I'm sitting in my own wee! What a date. I have to go. I'm so embarrassed."

"No, don't go," I said. "Look, it's okay. These things happen. At least you didn't poo."

"He is such an idiot," said Forest.

"Utter muppet," agreed Roger.

Helen sneezed again.

This was turning out to be one of those days. One of those lives.

"Can we all relax? And can everyone please just go to the bathroom if they need to?" Kale dashed out the back into the small garden behind the shop, Roger and Forest barged each other until Forest got into the compact bathroom first, and I turned to Sheila and Helen rabbit and said, "They have no manners. I was going to say ladies first."

"Boys will be boys," said Sheila. "You'll help?"

"Of course."

"What about your date with this lovely one?" she asked, stroking Helen.

"I think I blew it. I really like her, but look at what she walked into. If I had any sense, I would have called her when you turned up and told her to postpone the date for half an hour or so. I got caught up in things and now she thinks I'm a right idiot. Who needs this kind of grief? No offence."

"It's not your fault she turned into a rabbit," said Sheila, staring at the bunny and shaking her head. "My, what a strange town this is."

"You don't know the half of it. But we'll help you. Someone murdered your husband, so we need to find out who."

"Should we tell Chief Calum?"

"I don't think there's much point. We have history, and it's not a good one. He won't listen to either of us right now. But we need to tread carefully. If someone's out to get you too, then you need watching. No going off alone. Not even for a pee."

"You aren't coming in with me!"

"I mean, someone needs to be close by. To guard you. Kale can do that, can't you, boy?" I asked as he came running back in.

"I'll rip their knackers off if anyone tries anything," he said.

"If they have knackers," I reminded him.

"What was that about knackers?"

"I was talking to Kale. He's my familiar. He talks to me."

"Of course he does," chuckled Sheila.

The guys returned from their bathroom break and I gave them an ear-bashing. "Ever heard of manners? You two stormed off, even though Sheila here said she needed to go. You should know better. If Captain knew what happened, you'd be in a world of trouble."

"Don't tell him," said Forest, panicked.

"Sorry Sheila, we were being dumb," said Roger.

"You boys and your willies," she said, shaking her head.

I had no idea what she meant, and absolutely was not going to ask.

"I want a big fry-up tomorrow, or else," I warned them both.

"Sneak."

"That's blackmail."

"Deal with it," I grinned.

Sheila placed Helen rabbit on the table and went to use the facilities.

"We need to get you lessons," I told her. "We can help guide you through this. Help your witch gifts to manifest. Or maybe it's better if we find a witch to teach you. You can't keep doing this. You look cute, but it's inconvenient, right?"

The bunny sneezed and there she was, somehow cross-legged and looking dishevelled and all kinds of hot. "Lessons would be great," she admitted. "Oh, and don't worry, I don't think you're an idiot."

"You heard that?" I asked.

"Of course. Rabbits have good hearing."

"I just figured you couldn't understand. You don't normally when you shift. You become the animal."

"Not when it's for a brief period," said Forest. "It takes a while to settle into the form."

"Great, now I actually have blown it."

"No, you haven't." Helen slid off the table, smiled sweetly, and pecked me on the cheek. A deep scent of apples, grass, and honey was stronger than ever, as if the excitement had caused her to figuratively blossom. I wanted to lick her, but figured that really would blow it. "Today may be rather, er, unconventional, but it isn't your fault. You even did a hamper. I saw it in the shop. That is so sweet." She kissed me on the cheek again and smiled wider.

"I think you'll be making the breakfast tomorrow for everyone," crowed Roger, then zipped his mouth signalling he wouldn't spill the beans about the hamper.

"You got it!" I didn't care. Main thing was, I hadn't made an utter mess of things.

"But today, we need to help Sheila," said Helen.

"Me and the guys will help her. You don't want to get involved."

"We're a team, right?" she asked, all smiles and even more excited about this than my housemates.

"A team," said Forest, grinning.

"None of us know the first thing about hunting down a murderer," I protested.

"Course we do," said Roger. "We've solved half the crimes in town these last few years. Calum's stretched too thin. He only has three officers, and we help out. Not that he thinks so. But we're good."

"The best," agreed Forest.

"We figure out easy stuff, not murders. And it's dangerous. Someone got killed. No, Helen, I'm sorry, but it's too risky." I looked around but she wasn't there. "Where'd she go?"

"I think she went to buy a baseball bat," laughed Forest.

"Really?"

"No, you idiot, she's gone to check out the hamper."

I groaned. From looking forward to spending quality time with Helen, I was now up to the elbows in people and mystery and there was a good chance my date would be dead before we even got a chance to have a sandwich.

"Everyone ready?" asked Sheila as she emerged from the bathroom.

"As we'll ever be," I said.

"That's the spirit." Sheila marched out into the shop.

"Are we really doing this?" I whispered to the guys.

"Do we have any choice?" asked Forest.

"Doesn't look like it."

"Then let's make it awesome!" said Roger.

"I'm getting a new lodger," I sighed.

"Will you stop calling me that! I'm your cousin. You'll give me a complex."

"There's nothing complex about you," joked Forest as we went to join the ladies.

I grabbed my staff before we left, then blew out the candles. We took the hamper, but it was wishful thinking.

I forgot to have a pee.

The Past Revealed

The drive didn't take long, although it was rather a squeeze for those in the back. The Land Rover is roomy, but there are still limits. Kale takes up enough room for two adults on his own. Anxiety threatened to overwhelm me as old wounds surfaced, the memory of the crash, of how I couldn't even sit in a car for a year.

The first time I drove again was when I came home, and I took it slowly through the lanes. Subconsciously, I'd taken a route that led me directly past the crash site. I sat there for an hour, going over and over it, wondering what I could have done differently. But there was nothing. I saw the JCB, I broke hard, the brakes locked up, and I skidded right into it.

For another year or more after that I drove little, always with an anxious knot in the pit of my stomach, but I faced my fears, and gradually I learnt how to enjoy our country lanes. With Helen and Sheila in the back, the fear was trying to bubble to the surface, but I refused to let it. I was in control. I was not afraid.

Arriving was still a relief, even with what we would face next.

"Do not," I warned, "laugh."

"Why would I laugh?" asked a confused Helen.

"You'll see," I said grimly. "Shall we do this?" I asked the others.

"Yep," said Roger.

"No time like the present," agreed Forest.

"Sheila, this will seem beyond strange to you. Please don't be alarmed, and please don't think we're joking either. It's how we work," I said, sounding like this was something we did all the time. Okay, we do it quite often, but not to discover how someone was murdered.

Helen and Sheila stood away from us as instructed while Kale went sniffing about the loose rock and shale. We each removed our gear from our packs and put on our cloaks, then our hats, and gripped our staves tight. I felt like an utter idiot. It had taken some convincing to get me to wear the stereotypical wizard outfit when I came back home, but the truth was once I did, I experienced the increase in my abilities. There was no denying that these ancestral artefacts held not just meaning and memories, but the power of our male ancestors.

I turned to Helen and Sheila, who were watching with their jaws slack, utterly bewildered.

"You aren't serious?" asked Helen.

"Oh, how wonderful." Sheila clapped her hands in delight as we adjusted our hats and cloaks.

"Look, I know it seems ridiculous, but these things have power. They were our ancestors', and they're full of magic. Brimming with power. This hat is so soaked in spells and spilled potions it's almost sentient. Actually, it is," I admitted, although I didn't tell them it was also annoying once it started banging on about heads.

"Really?" giggled Helen, then turned to Sheila and said, "Sorry, I know this is to find out what happened, but look at them."

"I think they look lovely. Very smart," said Sheila.

"Thank you." I turned my attention back to Helen. "Bet this isn't the date you expected."

"Not exactly," she said, eyes dancing with amusement she was trying, and failing, to hide. "It really works? You guys really are wizards? And does Kale talk to you? Can you understand him?"

"Helen, if I may interrupt," said Roger as he stepped forward with Forest. "You do remember that yesterday you sneezed and turned into a cute bunny, don't you? Then you did it again today and weed over poor Sheila here."

Helen reddened and stammered, "Yes, but that was, er... This is different. You're all... And Besides, that was because of... Oh, fine, you got me." She laughed nervously, then frowned and asked, "Have you guys done this before? And what exactly are you going to do?"

"We're going to join forces so we can recreate past events. We'll see what happened. I warn you both now, it won't be pretty. Sheila, you might want to look away."

"Dear, I was a nurse for thirty-seven years. I've seen worse than you ever will. I'll be fine."

"Don't say I didn't warn you. And there will be magic, and all kinds of weird stuff going on, so look out."

"What weird stuff?" asked Forest.

"There won't be, will there?" asked Roger.

"Won't there?" I was out of my depth now. They shook their heads. "Fine," I told the ladies, "there will be no weird spooky stuff, just a conjuring of the past made real."

"Sounds great," said Sheila, with a clap of her hands.

What was with her? She wasn't cut up about her husband, which was fair enough, although odd, but was she actually enjoying this?

I was already burning up in my cloak so told the guys, "Let's get on with it." With a nod to each other, we took our positions.

Getting used to the outfit is taking a while. In fact, I've never felt right donning this traditional garb. The hat is brown, crooked, way too tall, and smells funny. The cloak is drab, heavy, made of ancient itchy hessian, and neither long nor short enough. As for the staff, well, the staff is awesome. Whenever I pick it up, I feel great. Brimming with elemental forces. Able to channel the powers all around us into and through the ancient wood. It's warm, fits in my hand perfectly, and if I'm being honest, it actually makes me feel like a genuine wizard. I still look a first-class numpty though. At least I wasn't alone.

The midday sun pummelled us as we spread our arms wide and opened ourselves up to the power within and without. Gently, our staff hands moved forward until they pointed at the centre of our makeshift circle. The magic would be contained within it; we just had to remain focused.

When the chant was complete, we dropped our arms and let the past play out in real time.

At first the image was shrouded in ethereal mist, like looking through filthy glass, but then it cleared and became if not as crisp as reality, then close to it. The overlay of the past and present wasn't perfect, off by a foot or two, so it was like seeing double when you stared at the land. We looked up, and there at the cliff's edge I made out... Nothing.

Suddenly, a man came sailing over the edge, arms flailing, screaming as he plummeted. Then he smashed into the ground, arms and legs akimbo, clearly dead.

Groaning, we lifted our staves, closed off the spell, and reality slapped back into existence with an annoyed grunt.

"Well, that was pointless," said Roger.

"Why didn't we do it up on the cliff so we could see how he fell?" I mused.

"You said we had to do it here," said Forest.

"I don't think I did. You were the one who said this was the best spot."

"No, it was definitely you. Or was it Roger?" asked Forest, glaring at him from under his misshapen, pointy hat.

"Stop bickering, you guys," shouted Helen.

We turned to her and I realised what we'd done. She was clutching tight to Sheila who was visibly shaking and very pale. Helen was crying.

"Damn, sorry. Are you both okay?"

"I've never seen a dead body before," said Helen. "That was awful."

"He's really dead?" asked Sheila, the truth finally sinking in.

"Yes. He is."

"Silly old bugger. I told him to be careful. But he always knew best. Now look what he's gone and done."

"We still don't know what happened. We'll go up onto the top and repeat the chant and then we'll know for sure. You can wait here if you like, or just look the other way."

"No, I want to see."

"I don't," said Helen, wiping her eyes.

Kale barked from the loose rocks at the cliff base. We turned and I called out, "What is it?" although I could just as easily have used telepathy. If we're within a hundred metres or so, then we can communicate just fine that way. Anything more and it's like talking on a phone with a bad signal. Something we are used to.

"Not sure. But there's something hidden here. Or buried." Kale began digging furiously with his massive paws, flinging shale and clumps of grass in all directions.

"He's found something," I told the others, so we rushed over as Kale moved to my right.

I threw rocks and earth aside as I uncovered a shining object. Was this is? The clue we needed to break the case wide open? How awesome would that be? I brushed the dirt off and groaned as I lifted the "clue" from the ground then turned to show the others. It was only then that I understood if it had been a real clue, then I shouldn't have touched it. It was evidence in a murder. The police needed to be here to do things properly.

"It's a Frisbee," said Forest. "I don't get it."

"What does it mean?" asked Sheila, still shaken.

"Nothing," I admitted. "It's just a Frisbee. Dog walkers lose them all the time. They come walking down here and lose them. Kale's always finding balls and other toys."

"It might be a clue," said Kale hopefully.

I patted him on the back and told him, "Well done for finding it, but I don't think so. You want to keep it?"

"Can we play?"

"Sure."

While everyone got over the disappointment, Helen and I snatched a few minutes to throw the Frisbee for Kale. He was so fast though that we managed mere seconds alone before he returned for another throw. This was not going well. Neither our date or the crime solving.

"We should go up to the bluff. Should have enough of a recharge by now."

"Does it work like batteries, then? You have to top yourself back up? How does that work?"

"I have to bask in the presence of beauty," I said, serious.

"You are such a charmer, Bran Fairfield," she laughed, then stroked my arm.

Result! I was finally saying the right thing.

"Can I sniff her bum?" asked Kale.

"No bum sniffing," I blurted as I stared into Helen's eyes.

She burst out laughing, I put my head in my hands, and Kale ran off, tail swishing happily. He'd planned that, I was sure.

"I assume you were talking to Kale?" Helen asked.

"Yeah," I groaned. So much for Mr. Smooth.

"Come on, let's go catch us a murderer." Helen held out her hand and I took it without hesitation. The moment we touched, a jolt of energy zinged up my arm and lit my heart on fire. It felt like coming home.

"Feels like coming home," I sighed, unable to stop the words.

"My heart's melting," groaned Helen, squeezing tight.

We looked into each other's eyes and I just knew. She was the one.

"Come on, you two," shouted Forest. "We're melting in this heat. Get a move on." He must have realised we were holding hands and looking love struck, which is a real thing, so added, "But no hurry. Take as long as you need."

We smiled at one another then Helen said, "That was intense."

And then I ruined the moment by saying, "You ain't seen nothing yet." I groaned at my own stupidity as her eyes danced with mirth. "Sorry, I'm not usually this dumb."

"Neither am I," she admitted. "Come on, let's go watch an old man die. Again."

We trailed after the others who were already halfway up the steep walk to the top of the bluff.

"What is this place?" asked Helen as we slowly caught up.

"It's a former quarry. From hundreds of years ago. They dug it out for the rock to build some of the houses, most in fact, in town. There's a lot of magic here which makes our job easier. The woods grew up around it, and now it's popular with walkers. The view's great from the top. You can see half of England. Maybe not quite, but it's impressive. Down there," I pointed to the woods now beneath us, "is where loads of people park their campervans if the official campsite is full or they just don't want to pay. Others set up tents to camp in the woods. Some have been there for years. It's like another town within a town."

"And they're allowed to?"

"Sure. Why not? It's good for the town, means more people use the shops. If they behave then what's the harm?"

"That's very liberated. Most towns hate travellers or anyone parking up on private land. You have to use the campsites."

"And a lot do. But it gets costly. And the woods are special. Very old. The heart of it is ancient. These smaller trees are only a hundred or two years old, but down lower, where most people set up, it's truly old. I'll have to show you some time."

"That would be lovely."

We caught up with the others so reluctantly let each other go, only then realising we were still holding hands. I felt like part of me was missing immediately. This was real scary stuff. Was I enchanted, or just enamoured? I didn't care. I felt awesome.

After a hard slog up the winding path, we reached the top. Sheila was the only one not out of breath.

"You all need to get more exercise," she admonished. "More walking."

We mumbled that we would, so she marched off ahead and we followed, suitably chastised. Several minutes later, we were approaching the right place, with the countryside open around us. The view breathtaking.

After milling about for a while, I got a tingle and looked up to find the guys had stopped too. "This is the spot," I said.

They both agreed.

"He fell from here?" asked Sheila, guided by Helen to stand beside us.

"This is as close as is safe. We'll need you both to move far back so we can do things properly this time." They both nodded, and it was only then I realised I and the guys were still wearing our wizard clothes. I guess if Helen could fall for me dressed like a sack of potatoes with a pointy end then I was definitely onto a winner. Trying not to look too happy about life, I nodded to the others and we picked up our positions once more.

We repeated the chant and the actions, and the air became fuzzy. Haltingly, through the murk, a figure appeared. As the images sharpened, Sheila gasped at the sight of her husband. He was marching along the path, a safe distance from the edge. Suddenly, he turned and shouted something angrily then continued his walk. Again, he stopped and turned, then he waited as a figure emerged from the blurry edges.

The man wore a green jacket favoured by hikers for its lightweight but waterproof abilities, perfect for getting caught in a sun shower on a warm day. The hood was up and his head was down as he glanced around furtively, clearly checking if there were others on the bluff. I peered forward, trying to intensify the power I was providing for this conjuring, and I felt the energy from the others as we strained to get a good look at the man.

The focus began to sharpen as the two men drew closer.

This was it. We'd have our answer. I held my breath as the man stepped right up to Albert. He raised a hand to brush back his hood and—

"What the hell do you think you're doing?" shouted Police Chief Calum Swift at just about the worst possible moment.

Images from a past it was impossible to change blew away on a magical breeze, leaving nothing but wisps of fuzzy memories in their wake.

The spell was broken.

Angry Words

We turned to see Calum storming towards us, smart and official in his dark uniform, hat held under his arm, every ounce the angry local copper. "After last night, I can't believe you're putting this poor woman through this, Bran. Shame on you."

"We're helping her find out who killed her husband," barked Forest, stepping up to him and matching his angry stare.

"It's okay, Forest, let me handle this," I said.

"You sure?" he asked, turning back to Calum and puffing out his chest.

"Yes. We don't want this to get out of hand."

Forest stepped away and Calum turned to me. "Looks like it's already out of hand. You know better than this, Bran. Or I thought you did. I told you, it's done. Over. He slipped. It's a dangerous spot. Look, the edge is crumbling." Right on cue, a small patch of grass and earth overhanging the quarry fell away and tumbled to the ground below.

"Sheila told us, same as she told you, that Albert was a cautious man. Never went close to the edge. No way he could have fallen."

"He was on medication. He probably had a dizzy spell, got disorientated, and slipped."

"That's what I said too. But Kale and I did a reading, Calum, and there's no doubt in my mind he was pushed. If you hadn't interrupted us, we would have seen the killer. We were in the middle of a conjuring to see what happened. There was definitely someone with him. We all saw it. Now it's gone and we'll never know."

"What do you mean, we'll never know?" shrieked Sheila. "We saw that man. He must have been the one. You can do it again and we'll finally see who he is."

"Sorry, but no, we can't," said Roger, looking as annoyed as I felt. "It's a one-time thing. You can only see the past once, otherwise people would be spending their whole lives obsessing over their lost loved ones. We had our chance, and someone blew it." Roger didn't even turn to look at Calum, but we all knew who he meant.

"You... you really saw?" he asked, frowning, his posture relaxing.

"Yes," I said. "There was a man with Albert. They were shouting at each other. He had his hood up. We were a second away from seeing him, but now it's gone." I removed my hat, pulled off my cloak, and stuffed them into my pack, relieved to be out of the itchy garb. Roger and Forest did the same, and we took a moment to recover from what was quite an energy draining act of magic.

"I didn't know. I thought you were trying to convince Sheila. Or get her to admit to it. After yesterday when you told me you thought she might have done it, and I saw you all here..."

"You what? Thought we were bullying her into an admission? Come on, Calum, that's not us. That's not me."

Calum ran a hand over his sweating head and nodded. He turned to Sheila and said, "Sorry. I just saw you all and, well, I figured they were up to something."

"The only thing they were up to was solving this murder. Something you seem utterly uninterested in doing, Police Chief Swift. They were helping. And they're such lovely people too."

"We are lovely, aren't we?" joked Forest. I shot him my best evil wizard stare, but he just smirked.

"That's why I'm here. I don't take these things lightly. After I spoke to you earlier, just to check on what Bran told me, I got to thinking. I'm not saying I believed it was murder, but I figured another look at the scene wouldn't hurt."

"And now?" she asked.

"If you say you saw a man with your husband, and I don't doubt you did, then I guess it warrants further investigation."

"Warrants further investigation?" she asked, incredulous. "Is that police talk for we might look into it a bit? Or does it mean you'll catch the killer?"

"It means," he said gruffly, "that I'll look into it until I'm satisfied. I can't call in detectives for this though. Someone already came yesterday and they were happy to call it death by misadventure. If I want them back, we need more. And that isn't me telling them a bunch of shop-owning, dodgy builders who dress up in pointy hats saw the victim talking to somebody at an unspecified time before he fell to his death. Understand?" he asked, staring at me and the guys.

"We understand," I said.

"Well I don't," said Helen. "We just told you what we saw. It was moments before his death, and he was with a man. They were arguing. Isn't that proof enough?"

"It's no proof at all," said Calum. "And like I said, I can't go telling anyone that you saw it because of a conjuring. This town's already the laughingstock with the other departments, all the nonsense that goes on here. They don't believe. I do. Which is why I'm willing to look into it, but you better let me do my job. No more interfering," he warned.

"We're going to help Sheila," Helen told him, defiant.

"Who are you?" asked Calum, looking ready to burst a blood vessel.

"I'm Helen Granger. I just moved back with my mum."

"Little Helen Granger? I remember you, and your mum. Sorry to hear about your gran. She was a good woman. A powerful witch. Quite a reputation." He smiled, clearly remembering some of her antics. "But that doesn't mean you can interfere. You're disturbing a crime scene."

"Thought there was no crime?" asked Roger.

"Maybe," he growled. "Just let me do my job."

"Yes, Chief Swift," said Sheila demurely, looking suddenly like a frail old woman.

Calum grunted his approval, so with a nod we wandered back along the path, leaving him standing there, looking lost and very alone.

"Poor guy," said Roger.

"Must be hard to be a policeman in this town," said Helen.

"You don't know the half of it. He believes, but he isn't gifted. His wife was, though. And his daughter."

"What were they like?"

"Another time," I said, not wanting to talk about it. Helen already knew my connection to Calum, so I saw no reason to sour the mood. And besides, we had more important things to think about.

We marched along behind Sheila, who seemed more determined than ever after our interruption. But I had no idea how to proceed, and neither did the guys. After a brief talk, we decided the best thing was to take Sheila back to her campervan and try to figure something out.

"No, we can't do that," I said, realisation hitting. "Remember what I said about the reading? Someone's out to get the poor woman. We need to keep her close."

"We still need to go see Helen's gaff," said Forest. "We promised her we would."

"And we can't babysit Sheila all day and night. Don't forget it's dart's night too," Roger reminded us.

"Do we have to?" I groaned.

"Yes, it's tradition. It gets our dads, and Captain, out of that house. They need to unwind. You know what they're like if they don't get their weekly fix."

"A nightmare. They go stir crazy and take it out on us."

"Exactly."

"Then I have the perfect solution," I said with an evil grin.

"Are you thinking what I'm thinking?" asked Forest.

"Oh yes," I said.

Brave Girl

"My van!" shrieked Sheila from the back seat. "Someone's stolen my campervan. Stop the car."

I pulled in and parked; Sheila was out of the Land Rover before I even had a chance to switch the engine off.

"Where's she going?" asked Helen.

"I have no idea, but we need to get her. She's in shock I think. How would she know someone's stolen her van?"

We ran after her down the street, turned a corner, and almost slammed into her. She was standing beside a campervan, confusion evident.

"It looks just like ours. I could have sworn it was. Same colour, same make. It even has the little red curtains, see. And the same sticker." Sheila rested a hand against the door, shaking her head in confusion.

I stared at the Little Hope sticker with the silhouette of a wizard's hat. Just like the one she'd bought from me yesterday. This was one of thousands I've sold over the years, but it was slightly faded so wasn't new.

"You sure it isn't your vehicle?" asked Helen.

"What? Oh, yes, of course. The registration is different. But for a moment there... Oh, it sounds so silly. I thought it was Albert driving and he was still alive. That there'd been a mistake."

"It's a stressful time," I said. "The mind plays tricks on you. You positive this isn't yours? Where did you park?"

"I left it at the campsite and walked into town. Didn't want to unhook everything after it's connected. I always struggle with the gas bottles. Albert always does the hook-ups. Oh dear, I don't suppose he ever will again."

Helen held on to Sheila as she sobbed. I told the guys that I needed to phone Dad to warn them and ask if it was okay to do what we'd discussed, so I dashed off to one of the nearest phone boxes to make a call.

People are so enamoured with the old-fashioned red phone booths that they actually take pictures. A real slice of British history. Now almost vanished from the rest of the country, we have scores of them dotted around town as they are the most reliable means of communication in a town where technology is almost a swear word.

I phoned home and Uncle Frank answered on the third ring. I told my uncle everything that had happened and asked if we could bring Sheila over. He said that would be fine, and that we should have told him what we were doing, but I explained it had all happened so fast and there hadn't been time. He was happy with the answer, but warned me that Captain might not be so easily placated. I didn't need telling that. But we had to keep Sheila safe, and what better place than in the company of Captain? Nobody would dare touch her if it meant going through him.

When I returned, Sheila was looking much better and they were all discussing the campervan.

"There must be loads of them," said Roger. "I've seen a few and they're a good price, especially the second-hand ones. Last forever, these beauties. Can't go wrong with a Volkswagen Transporter."

"Sorry for being silly. When I saw the curtains, I just believed it was Albert driving."

"I'm guessing they came with the van?" I asked.

"Yes. I think they're very common with the people who fit out the interiors. You must think I'm a mad old woman."

"No, of course not," I said, putting my hand on her shoulder. "I've made arrangements for you to be safe until we can figure something out, so let's go get you settled with our dads and grandad. We have some things to do, but we won't leave you alone until this is settled, okay?"

"Thank you so much. You're all too kind. I don't deserve such help. And I'm ruining your day. You and this lovely girl had plans, and it's Saturday. You don't want to be chasing around town with a sad old woman in tow."

"It's our pleasure. Um, not pleasure, but we want to help."

The others murmured their agreement and we walked back to the Land Rover and piled back in.

A few minutes later, we were at the top of town and I parked outside the row of houses.

"Nice," said Sheila. "Which one is yours?"

I pointed it out and told her, "Forest and Roger did the renovations for all four houses. Helen wants her place looked at, so we're going to go over there for a while. Think you'll be okay with a bunch of old men and one really, really old man?"

"Even older than me?" she chuckled.

"Much. And a lot less pretty."

Everyone groaned.

"So lame," said Forest.

"Cheesy as cheese on toast with extra cheese."

"You could have just said a lump of cheese," I said.

"I like cheese on toast."

"Me too," said Forest.

"Can we stop talking about cheese?" I shouted. "Helen, can you help Sheila out?"

"Of course. You smooth talker, you." She winked and smiled at me as she opened the door. Once Helen and Sheila were out, Forest turned to me and said, "You lucky bugger. She's awesome. I saw the two of you earlier. You gonna marry her?"

"Shut up!" I snapped, grinning from ear to ear.

"Don't screw it up," warned Roger.

"Why would I?"

"We know you, Bran. You like to thrust a stick in the spokes of your own happiness. Believing you don't deserve any joy."

"I do not. I will not mess this up," I promised them. I promised myself too. "Just make sure you give her a good deal on the renovations."

"Mates rates?" they asked, aghast. Roger visibly blanched, Forest swallowed a bit of sick.

"Mates rates," I nodded.

"We were already going to give her a good price, but c'mon. We like her, but there are limits."

"Mates rates. No discussion. Right, let's get this over with."

Before we were at the door, Uncle Frank opened it and rushed down the steps. "My dear lady, so sorry to hear about your loss. Come in, come in. You must be exhausted." Uncle Frank took her arm and led a bewildered Sheila into the house.

"Guess we're allowed in too," I told Helen, who was looking a little freaked out. "Don't worry, they're all like that. He probably didn't even see you. Uncle Frank gets too focused sometimes, if you know what I mean."

"Not really," she said, looking like she was ready to bolt.

"Do you want to wait in the car? Maybe you should. They can be rather intense, and I didn't exactly plan to bring you to meet the family on a first date."

"No, it's okay. I, um, I'm actually nervous. Can you believe it? So silly. I'm a proper grown-up. At least, I think I am." Helen laughed, clearly uncomfortable.

"No, entirely justified," I said, then took her hand, felt that zing of static, and smiled.

We followed Forest, Roger, and Kale into the house.

I showed Helen the way to the kitchen, where we usually congregate. When we entered, everyone was standing by the table, staring.

"What?" I asked.

"You had a date," scowled Dad, "and you didn't tell us."

"I told you yesterday."

"No you didn't. We'd remember."

"He did," said Forest. "We all did."

"You just forgot," said Roger gently. "Sometimes you forget things."

"And you had a murder and didn't tell us about that either."

"I told you last night that I had to see Calum as I'd told Sheila here to push her husband off a cliff. The rest has just happened today."

"You snitch," hissed Captain.

"I am not a snitch. I was just making sure Sheila didn't off her husband. No offence."

"None taken," she said, smiling with sympathy.

"Nobody likes a snitch. And does she look like a murderer?" asked Captain.

"Who knows," I shrugged. "Again, no offence."

"And none taken again."

"Take a seat, you poor thing," said Captain, pulling out a chair and scowling at the rest of us. "Someone here has manners. Would you like some lasagna? We have a big block in the freezer. Or how about a nice cake? Frank can bake a cake, and they're almost edible. Or how about I cast a spell to make you forget all about this nasty business?"

"No spells!" we all shouted, making Helen and Sheila jump.

"Fine, no spells." Captain winked at Sheila as he adjusted his fedora.

Kale barked, then went for a rest by the Aga.

"Who's this?" asked Captain, staring myopically at Helen. "Why is she blurry? Have you done something to her? Is it a girl?"

"Dad, put your glasses on," said Dad, handing them to Captain.

"Call me Captain," he growled.

"Everyone, this is Helen. Remember, I said I had a date with her today? It, er, went rather wrong, and we ended up trying to figure out who killed Sheila's husband."

"Hi." Helen waved nervously, then gulped. "Do not sneeze, do not sneeze," she mumbled under her breath.

"Pay no attention to this lot," said Dad, winking at me and grinning so wide he looked like he was about to swallow his own face. "You're very pretty. Well done, Bran."

"I didn't have anything to do with it. She was born like that."

"And what a smile. Those dimples! You could rest marbles in them. Or peas."

"Even small nuts," said Uncle Frank. "Or raisins."

"Why are you going to stick marbles to her face?" asked Captain. "And don't you go assaulting her with dried fruit. Remember last time? Give her a chair. Poor thing looks like she's about to collapse. Don't they feed you at home? Are you ill? Give her some lasagna. Frank, get the Aga firing. Jin, you're the better baker, and this stick thing needs cake. Me too. And a cuppa would be nice. None of that tea in triangle bags. I want square ones. It tastes wrong in triangles. How's the flavour meant to get out the top when it's all pointy? Stupid idea. Don't know what's wrong with them these days."

"Who?" I asked, unable to stop myself when I really do know better.

"The idiots who put tea in triangles."

"It's still just tea, isn't it? How does it taste different?" asked Helen.

The room went silent, Captain's eyes narrowed, looking huge magnified by his glasses.

"Ah, now I get it," he said. "She likes you because she's a bit simple in the head." He cackled, nodding sagely.

"She is not! That's a mean thing to say, and very insulting."

"Watch your mouth, old man, or I'll rinse it out with soap," snapped Helen, glaring at Captain, somehow not turning to dust under his steely glare.

Everyone gasped, and then Captain removed his hat, rubbed his forehead, shook out his hair as it's his favourite way to annoy Dad and Uncle Frank, then leaned back and laughed uproariously. "I like her. Bran, go buy a wedding ring. She's a keeper. Finally, someone who has some mettle."

With the ice broken, and my admiration for Helen now in the stratosphere, we settled down to a cup of tea, some biscuits, and a lot of questions from the mad old codger. Captain hated being out of the loop, so we went over the whole sorry story, right up to the present.

When we'd finished, everyone waited while he hitched up his long johns, angled his hat, gripped his staff, and said, "You'll figure it out."

"That's it?" I asked. "That's your big reveal?"

"I never said I'd know who killed poor Sheila's horrible husband," he snapped.

"He wasn't that bad," said Sheila.

"Sounded horrible to me," said Captain. "Any more biscuits?"

We made arrangements with Dad and Uncle Frank to look after Sheila, then got out of there as fast as we could.

Back in the safety of the Land Rover, everyone sighed with relief, then we burst out laughing, the stress finding a way out.

"I can't believe you stood up to Captain like that," I said, full of admiration.

"You're lucky he didn't turn your hair white. Or give you a wart. Or worse. One time I brought a guy home and he told Captain he looked in his eighties," said Roger. "He shrank his hands. Poor man couldn't even pick up his tea. Took a week to grow back to full size."

"He didn't?" asked Helen, shocked.

"Sure did. Let's just say we aren't still together."

"I like him. He seems harmless enough," said Helen.

"He really isn't," I said. "He's unpredictable, a bit forgetful, and very demanding. We love him, but he's hard work sometimes."

"Will Sheila be okay?"

"Sure," said Forest. "Our dads will look after her. Don't worry. Now, let's go check out your place. See what we can do for you. Bran said we have to give you mate's rates."

"Aw, that's so sweet. Thank you." Helen pecked me on the cheek yet again. I practically glowed with smugness.

"Hey, you should be kissing us, not him. We're the ones who will be out of pocket."

"Let's discuss the work, and see if we're a good match first," said Helen. "I haven't even said if I want to employ you yet. And let's get one thing clear. I may be nice and friendly, and go along with your antics, but when it comes to business I'm a hard-ass. Got it?"

I didn't think it was possible for me to like her more, but I did.

The guys slumped back, shocked, and Roger muttered to Forest, "We're the ones who decide if we want to work for someone. Not them. We can take our pick of jobs. Doesn't she know how these things work? We're in demand. We're meant to make the rules."

"Quiet, she might hear you," said a worried Forest.

Helen and I giggled in the front. Although, I wasn't sure if she was serious or not. I think she was.

Gizza Job

Helen's gran was well-known and well-liked in town. Not a face as such, because she mostly kept to herself and, unlike so many other residents, wasn't a gossip. Her house was larger than most, but hadn't been touched in a very long time.

With Helen and her mum living away, and her on her own, it had slowly settled into the landscape as trees matured and rhododendrons took over the front and rear gardens. You could tell right away it could be a charming home again, but it needed serious work. A beautiful decorative Victorian red brick construction, it looked sound enough, but who knew what lurked inside?

As we stood outside, discussing the merits of double glazing and the benefits and drawbacks of combi boilers versus conventional boilers with hot water storage tanks, then moving onto the options of grey or black aluminium windows and doors or wood, the front door opened and a woman smiled at us. It didn't take a genius to know this was Helen's mother. They were very alike, even down to the dimples, her mother simply being an older version of her daughter. The blond hair was fading to a nice pale yellow, she had a good tan, and shapely legs. A trim figure in a white t-shirt splattered with paint.

"I would," said Forest.

"You would not," said Helen. "Last thing she needs is a toy boy. Keep your hands in your pockets. No, keep them where I can see them."

"I think you must be a dream," I said. "Nobody is this awesome."

"I've gone right off her," said Forest grumpily.

"Who are your friends?" called Helen's mum. "Have you been playing?"

"Mum, I'm in my thirties, remember? I don't go out playing."

"Everyone likes to play," she said, smiling at us.

"I could play with that. Any game she wants," said Forest.

"Easy," I warned. "You're coming close to just being a pervert. And you're gonna get slapped. I'll tell your girlfriend."

"Sorry, just joking around. No offence to you or your mum," he told Helen.

"Come on, I'll introduce you." Helen led the way up the steps to the front door and said, "Mum, this is Bran, the guy I went to meet at lunch. This is his brother, Forest, and their lodger, Roger."

"How come I always get introduced last? Especially when I'm the most handsome. And I am not the lodger!"

"You most certainly are," purred Helen's mum.

"The lodger?" asked Roger, confused.

"The most handsome, I think she meant," said Forest.

"You think so?" Roger asked Forest.

"No! Not me, her." Forest pointed at the bemused woman.

Helen rolled her eyes and said, "Guys, this is my mum, Saffron."

"What a beautiful name," said Forest, stepping forward by barging us out of the way and taking her hand then raising it and kissing it.

"My, what lovely friends you have," said Saffron, giggling.

"Yes, awesome." Helen gave Forest the daggers as he turned to beam at us, so he let go and cleared his throat.

"We've come to see what work needs doing. Got any pipes that need flushing?" he asked, smirking at us like he was hilarious. "Anything that needs seeing to, I'm sure I've got the tool for the job."

Saffron was beside herself, giggling away and blushing a little.

"Cool it," I hissed. "You're going too far."

"Just giving her the banter. They eat this stuff up," he whispered.

"I'll make sure your tool never works again if you don't stop being rude to my mother," Helen hissed, face serious.

Forest doesn't always know when to act sensibly, and sometimes gets into trouble because of his inappropriate choice of words. The sad thing is, it works more often than not, and to be fair, he can be a charmer when he wants to be. He seems to have this uncanny knack of knowing exactly how to behave around people, reading them easily and knowing how to best relate to them. Seemed that in this case, it was toilet humour and sexual innuendo. It never hurts that he has deep, pale blue eyes women of all ages adore.

"Sorry. I didn't mean to cause offence."

"Now, which one of you had a date with my daughter? I didn't catch Helen's rather hasty introduction."

I stepped forward and said, "That would be me, Mrs. Granger.

"Call me Saffron. Bran, how was your afternoon? You're back earlier than I expected."

"It didn't go quite according to plan."

"Does anything ever in this town?" She scowled, clearly not completely settled back into the ways of Little Hope. "Don't tell me, there was magic involved."

"You could say that. But mostly it was about a murder."

"A murder? Is it safe?" Saffron looked around, like there was a killer hiding in the bushes.

"It's safe, but we've been looking into it. Nothing to worry about though."

"Are you sure?"

"You're safe."

"Don't worry, Mum, it doesn't involve us."

"You were there too? Did you see it happen?"

"No, of course not. Um, not when it actually happened. But then me and the guys, and the dead man's wife, plus Kale, of course, we..." Helen paused, most likely realising this was no quick story to tell on the steps. "Come on, let's get you inside. We can talk with the guys about the renovations. You've got lots to ask, haven't you?" Helen guided Saffron inside, so we followed them in. I knew this wouldn't be quick, but I wasn't quite prepared for how long it took.

"Blimey, that was the longest it's ever taken just to be told what work needs doing," complained Forest, looking frazzled.

"Saffron's a talker, that's for sure," sighed Roger.

"She does love to chat. About everything. You guys going to take the job?"

They stared at me like I was an idiot.

"Of course we are. It's a massive amount of work. They don't seem short of a few quid, and it'll keep us busy for months. We can do smaller jobs on the side, but this will see us through until the end of the year. Do the outside stuff now while the weather's good, then move inside to tart it up as it gets colder. Perfect timing. That's what I think, anyway. Forest?"

"What? Yes, we'll do it."

"What's up with you?" I asked.

"Look." Forest pointed at a battered white van pulling up outside the Granger's.

"Marvin."

"That guy. He rubs me up the wrong way," said Forest.

"He does that to everyone. I haven't met a single person who likes him. But he still gets work. I don't know how he does it. You'd think with all the horror stories about him, nobody would let him over the threshold."

"He gets the second-homers, or the elderly who don't know he's trouble," said Roger, disgust evident.

We'd all heard the stories over the years of the way he took advantage of people living alone, or those who weren't as sharp as they were in their youth. He's a predator, pure and simple.

"Let's get in the Land Rover before he collars us," said Roger.

But it was too late. Marvin rolled out of his Transit van, looked up at the Granger's, sighed as he removed his wizard's hat, then scowled at us as he pounded over.

"You sneaky little shi—"

"Watch it," warned Roger.

"I don't need any advice from a nancy boy," he grunted.

"Seriously? We're doing name calling about who we happen to fancy now? Grow up, Marvin," I snapped.

"You bunch of weirdos swooped in on the poor woman and took advantage, did you? She's only just lost her mum. Shame on you." Marvin mopped at his red head with a dirty rag, then stuffed it into his saggy size forty-four waistband.

"That won't wash with us, Marvin," said Roger. "We were asked by Helen, her daughter, so we came around to give a quote."

"Bunch of sneaks. You can't have all the work, you know. What makes you think you're better than me?" Marvin hitched up his grubby jeans, scratched his ample belly, and tried to intimidate us by glaring. It made him look like a myopic football.

"Because at least a third of our work is fixing the shoddy job you did," said Forest. "We have a good reputation for a reason. We never have to go back. We take our time, do things the right way. Appointments are kept, sometimes we even arrive early, and we do what we say we will. We even return people's calls when they leave a message. You ever done that, eh?"

"My work's quality," he huffed. "But I can't be taking my time like you flock of fairies. It's just me and the young 'un doing the work."

"Enough with the insults," I warned. "Bit rich coming from you when your own son is gay."

Marvin was instantly on the defensive. "Don't you talk about my lad like that. He's having issues, that's all. He'll grow out of it."

"He's almost thirty!"

"It's a phase. He'll settle down with a nice gal soon enough."

"Whatever. We have to go. Things to do," I said.

"Better go and introduce myself then," he smirked. "See if I can beat your quote. You know I can."

"We haven't quoted yet," Forest said. "But it won't matter. We made an agreement. Saffron is a nice woman, and she knows proper builders when she sees them. Not ones who have to pretend to be a wizard to get work. That's not even a proper wizard's hat. Who has stars on their hat?"

"It's my angle," he grunted. "People love it. Makes the out-of-towners feel like they're getting a magical renovation. I'm still gonna offer my services. See if I can woo those pretty ladies. Lay on the charm."

"Yeah, good luck with that," I said. "Because trust me, you really will need magic if you think you're going to charm them."

Me and the others high-fived, unable to resist scoring a childish point against Marvin.

He scowled, then stormed off back to his van, before hitching up his jeans and approaching the house.

We left him to it. Helen and Saffron would make short work of Marvin.

"I don't like that guy one bit," said Roger once we drove off.

"Nobody does. And don't let him get to you." I focused on the road, but we were already almost home. Little Hope is not a large town.

"The gay thing? I don't care about that. You guys know I've never cared what other people think, and unlike what people like Marvin expect, I've never had much grief about being gay, even in school. You both know that. When everyone you know is weird, liking men seems a bit of a letdown. No, it's that he thinks it bothers me that bothers me."

"So it does bother you?" I laughed.

"No, I said it doesn't. Stupid insults don't bother me. It's the fact he thinks the insults bother me that bothers me."

"But that's why people insult each other. Because they think it will annoy or upset the other person."

"I know what I mean," he said, folding his arms in a huff.

"I get it," said Forest.

"You do?" I glanced in the rearview.

"Yes, of course." He was shaking his head and smiling at me. "I don't," he mouthed silently.

"What a day. I need a shower. I can smell myself and it isn't pretty."

"We can smell you too, Bran. That's the stress of your date."

"And the murder," I reminded Forest.

"Yeah, that too. What are we going to do? How do we sort this mess out? And are you sure I can't ask Saffron out? She's hot."

"No way. It would be beyond weird. Don't ruin this for me."

"I'm just messing with you, bruv. I'll wait until you and Helen get hitched, then get with her mum." He laughed, but I wasn't so sure he was joking. Forest likes women, and he likes them of all ages.

We were home soon enough, and once in the living room I sank gratefully into a soft chair. I was beyond exhausted. Using magic always takes it out of you, but it was more than that. It was this thing with Helen. I'd wanted it to be just the two of us, and instead she'd got roped into Sheila's problem, seen us perform magic, witnessed a murder, had to meet my family, and then introduce us to her mother. I couldn't believe she was keen on me after such a messed-up day.

And there was no kidding myself. She was interested. I didn't need to second-guess, or have doubts. She was an adult, and acted like one. No silly games, no angst, or pretending we couldn't read the signs even when it was made utterly obvious, and no stringing things out. We were both too old for that, knew what life was about, had been around and didn't play dumb. I loved that about her. She was a proper, mature woman and it was refreshing. Several women I'd dated had such little life experience that they were still like adolescents. Helen was different.

Even better, she could handle Captain. Anyone who has the nerve to stand up to him is a fine person in my book.

Forest and Roger banged about in the kitchen making drinks while I remained sunk into the chair, going over the day and wondering what the plan was. I knew it would come to me; I just had to wait for inspiration to hit. Since being back, I've discovered I have a real skill for solving problems. My brain acts like a sponge, soaking up information, letting it settle, then somehow shuffling the pieces about until I solve the jigsaw puzzle. Often it's when taking a nap that I figure things out. Either when falling asleep or on the cusp of waking, it clicks into place.

Of course, there have also been plenty of times when we just stumble across the truth by accident, or someone blurts something and it's as simple as a few direct questions and we have the answer. But me and the guys now have a reputation as the go-to gang for many of the issues locals face, and it's another reason why Calum hates me. I can't help it though. It doesn't exactly feel like a duty, but like giving something back to a community I left behind for so long. If they need me, I'll help, and Calum will just have to deal with it. If he could get over himself, we would actually make a good team. But the chances of that happening any time soon are zero.

He isn't usually put out by my involvement, because often it's for issues he never even hears about. People are loath to involve the police in their business, and besides, he and his team of three are up against it, having to deal with other towns in the area where there are a lot more serious crime issues. No, it's the fact he has to see me at all that he hates. Tough, because I'm going nowhere.

I thought back again to what he'd said about the car, and what Roger had told me. I wished Calum could move on, find some peace after all these years, but he'd keep on stewing on this until the very end. Maybe there's a way to put this to rest finally. But how?

Now wasn't the time. Sheila needed us, and I needed a cup of tea.

"Any nuggets of inspiration?" asked Roger as we sat finishing our tea.

"No, nothing," I said. "Something just isn't adding up here, but I can't figure out what."

"It'll come to you," said Forest brightly, never one to dwell on the negative. We have that in common, but he's so chipper at times Roger and I wonder if he's on medication.

"I'm not so sure. I don't know what to do next."

"What if it was just an accident like Calum said? Our Police Chief has a lot of experience, and from what you told us he sounded pretty sure." Roger sipped his tea.

"Does it feel like an accident to you?" I asked.

"No, but I haven't got the tingle like you say you get. This isn't so much our thing as it's yours. Sidekicks, remember? You're the sleuth."

"I'm starting to wonder if I am. Calum needs to get over himself and start taking this seriously. What if whoever did this does come after Sheila?"

"She's safe with our lot. Imagine anyone trying to get into that house? They'd wish they were never born."

We laughed at the thought. He was right. Sheila was where she needed to be.

A thought came to me, and I groaned.

"What?" asked Forest.

"It's Saturday, right?"

"Yeah, so?"

I waited while they both caught up.

"They wouldn't, would they?" asked Roger.

"Not with Sheila?" said Forest. "They know better than that. One of them will stay behind, won't they?"

"Seriously? You think?" I asked, knowing the answer.

"I'll ring them, just to make sure. But our dads won't be that daft. Captain, maybe, as he thinks he and all Fairfields are immune to danger, but... I'll just check." Roger rushed off to make the call while we waited. He didn't take long.

"You were right. No answer at home. So I tried you know where. And they're there. Sheila too. Apparently she just did karaoke."

"Guess we're off to the pub then."

Witch's Head

Every Saturday for as long as I can remember, the whole family has gone to The Witch's Head. Of course, in a town full of so many supernatural types and magic users, it isn't the only pub, but it is the one our family has basically sponsored for generations. The Wizard's Head is somewhere no self-respecting wizard ever ventures, and for obvious reasons. Several others cater strictly for tourists, but The Witch's Head is the real deal.

And The No Head is a pub for supernatural beings, although it welcomes all magic users. I've only ever been there once, and it took me days to recover.

That our dads and grandfather wouldn't miss their night out should have been a given, but we'd foolishly forgotten just how seriously they took their fun. Tradition is important, so even if they had to crawl there when in the throes of a flu epidemic, they would. And did. Dad had once won darts night when he had a foot infection so bad he had to stand on one leg all night, a terrible cold, an ear oozing green gunk, and Captain had made an eye swell up so bad he couldn't see out of it because Dad had dared question the props department of The X-Files.

"I'm about as in the mood for this as a marathon session in front of the TV with Captain," I told the guys.

"It'll do you good. And besides, we have to go because otherwise Sheila might get murdered," said Forest, grinning from ear to ear.

"Oh, thank you very much for that. It helps so much."

"My pleasure. Come on," he said brightly, "go get cleaned up and changed."

"Maybe you could ask Helen?" suggested Roger.

"No chance! She's had more than enough of us for one day. If not a lifetime. I wouldn't be surprised if she never wants to see any of us again after today's fiasco."

"She wants to," said Forest.

"She does, doesn't she?" I said, smiling despite what lay ahead this evening. "Why don't you ask your boyfriend, or your girlfriend," I teased them both, grinning wickedly.

They took a step back in horror. "You know what happened last time," wailed Roger. "Captain started asking all those personal questions and Gavin was so embarrassed. Then Captain began... No, I can't even say it. And Dad wasn't much better."

"I'm keeping my lady away from them for as long as possible. I like her, so no way am I introducing her to the family," said Forest.

"But it's okay for Helen?"

"She's already met them now. She knows what she's letting herself in for. And besides, she can handle Captain. Never thought I'd say that about anyone." Forest seemed pleased with his answer, and he was right to be.

"And you never know," said Roger, "inspiration might hit. Sometimes the best ideas and revelations come when you forget your problems for a while."

He was right, but I still wasn't keen. The day had been enough for me to handle. I needed quiet alone time to recharge my magical and emotional batteries. Being around people all day and especially when emotions run high takes so much out of me.

With little choice unless I wanted the guys to be in charge, I went for a shower.

The Witch's Head was buzzing, same as always. The steamed windows gave no clue as to the madness that awaited inside, but the noise did. Think fifty wizards plus drink. That's about all you need to know. Oh, plus one grieving widow.

As we entered, the usual cacophony of wizards droning on about wands, spells, the best wood for staves, and the usual gossip assaulted my eardrums like Captain when his beloved TV burst into flames. It was his own fault, but it didn't stop him from wailing, and breaking all the windows. Of course, the main topic was Sheila, but my love life came a close second. As everyone slowly registered that we were here, a hush came over the assembled bunch of town misfits, to be quickly replaced with questions, opinions, recommendations for what shirt I should wear next time, and even several one-liners some of the younger guys thought might help me to woo her. I smiled politely, made chit-chat, and cautiously worked my way towards the bar.

Dad, Uncle Frank, Captain, Sheila, plus Helen and her mother, Saffron, were sitting around a table by the wall. I almost ran out screaming, but steeled myself, ignored the jibes from Roger and Frank, and waved at Helen before turning to the bar and waiting to get served. One thing was sure, tonight I would be having a beer or two. Often, I didn't bother at all, preferring to have a clear head in the morning, as using a quick spell never works the same as just not drinking, but one or two wasn't going to hurt.

"Yes?" asked John, standing there looking vacant as always. His arms hung limp by his sides, dark rings around his eyes making him look like a sickly, malnourished panda with his pale, almost translucent skin. Gladys, his wife of seven hundred years, stood behind him and slightly to one side, just as animated.

"Three pints, please, John," I said brightly, "and same again for whatever everyone had at the table."

"Anything... else?" he drawled, fangs making him lisp somewhat.

"That's it. How's business?" I asked, just for the perverse pleasure of waiting for an answer from the only resident male vampire, his wife being the only female. None of the others over the centuries had got on here, what with the killing and draining of blood. Left a sour taste in the mouth, if you know what I mean.

"Business is... fine. But I... prefer... the... hallowed months. We can... open up... earlier... then."

"Of course. Well, it'll soon be winter. Dark early, wet, cloudy, miserable. Cold. Long nights, short days."

"I... can't... wait." I think he tried to smile, but it just came across like he was straining to do a standing vampire poo. Not that I imagine it's any different from a regular poo. Although I absolutely do not think about these things. Why would I?

Waiting for John and Gladys to serve you, the most unlikely names for vampires ever, is almost a lesson in Zen meditation. They insist on keeping their original names, saying it helps them to fit in, but usually vampires call themselves something beginning with V once they're turned. Like Vasagil or Valdemel, although come to think of it they sound more suited to topical creams for intimate parts. At first you're practically willing them to get on with pouring the drinks or handling the beer pumps, and to hurry up and say what they're going to say, but over time you get into the spirit of it and find yourself relaxed and enjoying the silence between words. At least I do.

I know for a fact it drives Roger nuts and Captain point-blank refuses to talk to either of them. But that might be because back in the mists of time, they might have accidentally tried to drain one of our ancestors, and as Captain likes to say, "A Fairfield never forgets." Doesn't mean he'll drink anywhere else. The Wizard's Head isn't called that for no reason, and the animosity there is much more recent and a lot darker.

"Gladys will... get your drinks. Take... a... seat."

I nodded my thanks, then ignored the smirks and advice from the locals and waded through the air thick with half-formed spells, shuffling reluctantly over to the table.

"Hi everyone. Helen, Saffron, Sheila. I wasn't expecting to see any of you here." I raised my eyebrows at Helen, and she smiled, or maybe grimaced, as her mother answered.

"Your lovely Uncle Frank came over to introduce himself and suggested we might like to come along for a drink. Get to know everyone. It's, er, very colourful in here. We've never been before. And loud. The owners are... Oh, gosh, I almost said something I shouldn't." Saffron giggled into her half pint of what looked like a Martini complete with olive. John and Gladys aren't big on fancy glasses. They're proper old school and haven't quite caught up with what they call, "Modern... ways... of... doing... things."

"Wasn't that nice of Uncle Frank?" I hissed, shooting him daggers.

He raised his almost empty pint and said, "Cheers. My pleasure," before sliding closer to Helen's mum.

"Sheila, how are you holding up? Are they looking after you?" I asked.

"Oh yes," she giggled, sloshing what seemed to be a pint of pink Cava over Dad's legs. Served him right. "I'm having a lovely time. My poor Albert would have hated this," she confided, before gulping wine and humming to herself.

I shook my head at Dad and Uncle Frank, but they just smiled, bleary-eyed and oblivious. They keep forgetting that not everyone can say a few words before they go out for an evening and there will be no hangover in the morning. They should certainly have known better than to let everyone have such large drinks, especially so early in the evening. If I didn't curb it, everyone would be hammered before nine.

As Gladys parted the sea of wizards like she had the plague, and teetered over on high heels, carrying the tray of drinks, I realised my mistake. I'd ordered another round for everyone. Not good.

"Here are..." Everyone leaned forward, waiting for her to finish her sentence and put the tray down, "your..." The tray was almost on the table now, and Helen, Sheila, and Saffron craned further forward, willing her to finish, "drinks!" said Gladys, triumphantly. If you can say zero emotion, or even a flicker of awareness she was doing anything at all, counts as triumph.

"Thanks Gladys," said Forest happily, snatching up a pint and taking a deep drink. "Have one for yourself."

"Thank..." The pause went on so long that we all faced her and waited with bated breath, "you."

She turned and left, slowly parting the wizards as they felt her presence like spiders crawling around your neck.

Still standing, I took my drink and sipped it, trying to catch Helen's eye. But Forest had her attention as he chatted away, and she was jammed in between Dad and Saffron so I had to sit next to Roger and Sheila, trying to keep some distance from Captain as he insists that he has to dress up for darts night so always wears his cloak. He's never let it be washed, and it's older than him, so the more space the better. He's certain it will lose its magic that has built up over the generations if it's cleaned, when the rest of us know that all it will lose is its stink.

Familiar faces glanced our way continuously. We were, after all, the talk of the town. Murder was exciting for the residents, especially when it was an outsider and they hopefully had nothing to fear for themselves. But there was an edge tonight, as however much everyone acted like we were all untouchable, the truth was we knew it could have been a local who committed the crime.

News had obviously spread about Sheila's Tarot reading and our subsequent magic. You can't keep what you had for dinner secret in a place with so much past. I heard grumbles about Calum's lack of interest, others speaking up for him, saying he had a lot to cope with and was understaffed. Some defended his position, saying there was still no proof, but the overall consensus was that there was a murderer loose in our midst and the sooner he, or she, was caught, the sooner everyone could get back to inflicting harm on each other of a less final nature.

All of the gossip was caught in snippets, nobody came and said anything outright, but soon enough the conversations settled down into the more mundane, like who would win the darts match and was it worth risking a kebab or a burger once it was closing time. On that, the voices were unanimous. Closing time, after a fair few bevvies, was absolutely the only time you'd risk getting takeaway from Clem's.

"His coat!" shrieked Sheila, standing suddenly, almost knocking the table over. Everyone grabbed their drinks, but not before beer, wine, and other more esoteric alcoholic beverages spilled onto the always sticky floor.

"Whose coat?" asked Helen.

"Albert's. He bought a new coat."

"Okay, calm down, Sheila, and speak quietly. You don't want everyone to hear your business. Come outside for a moment," I said softly, thinking the fresh air would clear her head anyway. I wouldn't mind some peace either. It was ridiculously loud in here tonight, and I wasn't particularly in the mood for the gossiping and glances.

"I'll come with you," said Helen, then took Sheila's arm and helped her navigate the complexities of tables and chairs without getting stuck to the floor.

It was no mean feat. Several customers have been found the next day stuck fast to a particularly dodgy spot, John and Gladys seemingly having forgotten about them and just, "Gone... out... for a... nice... midnight walk."

Outside in the beer garden at the rear of the pub, we guided Sheila over to a picnic bench and helped her sit. She swayed slightly as she hummed along to music only she could hear.

"I think she's had too much to drink," said Helen.

"It's a possibility," I said, smiling.

"Okay, she definitely has," laughed Helen, that twinkle in her eye.

"I'm surprised you came. Thought you would have had enough of us by now."

"I wasn't going to. I didn't want to intrude, but Mum said she was coming, so I figured I'd better tag along to keep an eye on her. Plus, I did have an ulterior motive." Helen looked into my eyes and took my hand. We both gasped as the shock spasmed up our arms.

"I'm glad you did. You aren't running screaming for the hills yet, so that's a good sign."

"I'm hanging in there. Just. It's been a rather unconventional day. Is it always like this?"

"No, sometimes it's really mad," I said, not sure myself if I was joking or not.

"Wow, and you came back for this? You're a brave man."

"It's where I belong. It just took a while to realise that."

"I think I'm beginning to feel the same way. Especially now."

I gulped. Was she saying she meant because of me? "Especially now," I agreed.

"His jacket. And the new hat," shrieked Sheila, suddenly animated.

"What was that?" I asked.

Helen bent down and said, "Sheila, it's important you focus. What about the hat and jacket? Something to do with Albert?"

"Yes, he likes to shop. Liked to shop," she corrected. "You wouldn't think it to look at him, but he loved all the equipment. He adored the gadgets, and the walking gear. He went shopping. I think he bought more than he told me. Sometimes he even hides his purchases. But I know he bought a new hat and a new jacket. One of those breathable ones. They're supposed to stop you sweating or something. Is that right?"

"I think they just wick the moisture away," I said. "When was this?"

"The morning we got here. He went off on his own for a while. He always does. He had the jacket on when he died. Not the hat, but he had it on before he fell. Maybe someone knows something. Maybe you can find a clue."

"Maybe. Do you know where he bought them? And if he got anything else?"

"I don't think so. Not that I saw. But the hat was definitely new, and the jacket. He wore them both when he went out for his hike. I wanted to relax, I'm so tired. Oh, why did I let him go alone?"

"Sheila, listen to me," said Helen, taking her hands and waiting until Sheila focused on her. "It isn't your fault. If you'd been with him, you would have been in danger too. Bran will find out what happened, won't you, Bran?"

Both women turned to me with hope in their eyes. "I'll do my best," I promised.

"Thank you."

Dad came into the beer garden, eyes questioning. "Everything alright?"

"Fine. Sheila just remembered something, and it might help. I'll look into it tomorrow."

"Bran will find who did this," said Dad. "He's the best."

"Thanks, but I think you might be biased."

"Nonsense. You're a smart man, and I know you want to help Sheila. We all do. And Helen, it's been lovely meeting you and having you around. Your mum's a very special lady, too. Is she dating?"

I groaned. First Forest, then Uncle Frank, now Dad after Saffron too. It didn't bear thinking about.

"I, er, I don't think she's looking for anyone at the moment," said Helen.

"Oh, that's alright, neither am I."

"Good, because Mum isn't dead, remember? Just a hedgehog."

"Yes, of course," said Dad hurriedly. "Although it has been a while. Three years. A man has needs and—"

"Lalala, can't hear you." I covered my ears and glared at Dad. "She'll be back."

"I hope so." Dad didn't look that convinced by his own words.

"A hedgehog?" asked Helen.

"Long story."

"No it isn't," snapped Dad. "Stupid woman turned herself into a hedgehog and now she's stuck like that. She always was a meddler."

"Is a meddler," I corrected. "Because, like I said, Mum isn't dead."

"No, it just feels that way. Don't blame me, Bran, but sometimes I get lonely. It's hard without her being around."

"I know, but she'll be back." I turned to Helen. "Some witches can shapeshift, and we have a few proper shifters in town, too. Mum pushed beyond her limits and now she's stuck. We're all hoping she can shift back, but it hasn't happened yet."

"That's terrible. You aren't joking, are you?"

"No."

"This town is crazy." Helen shook her head at the sheer madness of it all. I didn't blame her. "Although, I guess I shouldn't be surprised. Not after my sneezing incidents."

"Come on, Sheila," said Dad, "let's get you back inside. The darts match is about to start."

"You sure that's a good idea?" I asked.

"Of course. Why wouldn't it be?"

"Oh, no reason," I laughed. "See you in a minute."

Dad led a wobbling Sheila away, leaving us alone.

"Your family are close, aren't they?"

"Very. But Mum and Dad had their problems even before she did this stupid thing. I know it sounds utterly ridiculous, but she really did shift and get stuck."

"I believe you, Bran. I'm beginning to realise the stories I heard from Gran weren't just tall tales. That magic is real and I'm a part of it. Always have been."

"Sneezing yourself into a bunny is definitely an awakening," I laughed.

"So your folks had problems?"

"Some. Same as lots of people do. They love each other, but Dad's not so great without some backup. It's why he's with Captain and Uncle Frank. I guess it's the same for me and the guys. We're better together. We look out for each other. Don't be scared off though," I blurted, hating the thought of this being too much for her to handle. "I can keep them at bay if they overwhelm you."

"I can handle it. I like it, actually. Everyone's so kind. Even Captain in his own way. Sort of." Helen giggled; we both knew he was a nightmare on bowed legs.

"I was really looking forward to today," I admitted. "More than I believed I could be."

"Me too. But there will be plenty of other days."

"I hope so."

"Come on, let's get back inside. I'm brilliant at darts, so prepare to get beaten."

"You don't stand a chance. Darts are in our blood. The Fairfields have been throwing pointy objects at things since we stepped out of the cave and began interfering with reality."

"Yes, but did you ever hit anything?" joked Helen.

"Sometimes," I admitted. "I'll be in soon. I just need a minute."

"Sure." Helen frowned, clearly wondering if everything was alright, but I nodded and smiled and she left me alone.

I breathed deep, the smell of the cut grass in the beer garden refreshing after the stink of inside the pub. John, the landlord, likes to mow the grass in the middle of the night—one of the ways he keeps busy and out of trouble —so it's always neatly clipped. The neighbours aren't too impressed, but nobody ever confronts him about it, because you don't, do you? Not when the landlord is a vampire and also happens to serve the best beer.

A few minutes of solitude was what I needed to recharge my energy enough to face the rest of the evening. Too much had happened, and far too fast, for me to keep up. Too many people, too much activity, too much chatter, and too much danger surrounding those I cared about. With this thing with Helen I was close to losing my grip on it all, almost overwhelmed with the intensity of the emotions. Could I really feel so much for her having just met her? I did, and that made me worry. Falling for someone like this wasn't good. No way could I get my heart broken again.

But what was the alternative? Shut myself off, try not to feel anything? That isn't me, and I hope it never will be. I'd cope, whatever happened. And I reminded myself that Helen and I had just met, that nothing had happened between us. Yet.

With a smile, I took a deep lungful of fresh air and went to throw pointy objects at a board with numbers on.

Wiping the Floor

Helen had gone by the time I went back inside. Had I said something wrong? Dad explained that Saffron was feeling rather tipsy, and Sheila too, so Helen and Uncle Frank had said they'd take them home.

Helen had told Dad to say goodbye, and that she was sorry, but we'd catch up soon. I hoped she meant it. Maybe it was for the best anyway, I decided. They'd all had more than enough of the local flavour for now, and although Helen and Sheila hadn't exactly been eased gently into our world, at least they'd been spared the raucous wizards in the pub once they really got going.

I actually felt relieved that she'd left once I thought about it. I didn't want to blow this, and my family barraging her with questions and sticking their noses into everyone's business was a sure way to put her off. They'd scared away plenty of love interests in the past for all of us, so this was good. No more bad impressions.

Captain drained his beer and stood, oblivious, or not caring, about the drinks he almost knocked out of people's hands as he stretched, readying himself for the big match. Dad was just as keen, performing his usual squats with his arms outstretched, although how that helped throw a dart I never have fathomed.

Forest and Roger were their usual quietly confident selves. Meaning, they were shouting abuse at the other teams and promising to wipe the floor with them. Yes, literally. Losers get dragged across the pub floor by the winning team. The Fairfields were on a roll, having not lost a match for three years ever since I returned home. It's why I'm stuck in this Groundhog Day of weekly darts matches—everyone insists I'm the good luck charm and if I wasn't here they'd lose.

Sometimes I grumble about coming, but mostly I enjoy it. It's fun, loud, wild, and dangerous, and you have to keep a careful watch for cheating. Wizards are renowned for using magic to give them a boost when competing, and this was about as serious as it got.

The room fell into silence as the teams assembled. We were up first, with Captain throwing three darts and then the other team taking their turn. Then we'd go through the other players in order. First team to go from five-oh-one down to zero are the winners, always having to finish on a double.

Captain skipped up to the oche, the throw line, and made a few practise movements to get the feel for the darts, then scowled at the other teams before throwing his first dart. He got twenty and muttered, then treble twenty and double top for his subsequent throws. Not bad at all. He jeered, and insulted the others as he stepped aside, leaning heavily on his staff until he took a seat to watch proceedings. He hates to admit it, but it takes it out of him.

The other team got a five, a triple twenty, and another triple twenty, much to the delight of the crowd. The third team bombed out with nothing of note, and then it was back to the Fairfields and my turn.

Maybe it was the tingle I'd had since meeting Helen, or maybe it was my good mood, or that I was simultaneously running through what Sheila had said about Albert's shopping obsession, but I felt clear-headed and in the zone, as though the darts knew the path they had to follow and I was merely a conduit.

I stepped up to the oche, confident and single-minded, empty of all distractions. I entered a quiet place where there was only me and the board, and I focused on the treble twenty. Grinning, and feeling beyond confident, I threw the darts one after the other, *thud, thud, thud,* hardly even looking at the board.

The crowd erupted as the umpire, namely John the landlord, shouted, "One hundred and eighty!" Suddenly the room went silent, then everyone went crazy, cheering for John as much as me as our landlord had never managed such a long sentence without pause in all his many centuries of unlife. Maybe my mood was catching?

With a pat on the back from my team, plus a slap across the rear of my legs from a cackling Captain, I stood aside and let the others try to claw back what I already knew was our inevitable victory.

When it came around to my turn again, after we'd already won the first game, I scored the same maximum score. It was incredible, and something I'd never achieved before. There were murmurs about cheating, but they were just sore losers, as everyone present had their feelers out. If anyone used magic, the whole room would know in an instant and your fate sealed.

We won the second game, and our unbeaten streak remained.

The losing teams were pulled across the soaked floor, then it was back to the business of drinking and gossiping, but by this time me and the guys had had enough and made our escape before the beer tempted us too much.

The thing I like the most about going to the pub is the walk home. There's a special atmosphere late at night in a place you know well. The quiet, if you leave before closing time, is beautiful after the hustle and bustle of the day. Sometimes there are a few locals walking dogs, or visitors just milling about, soaking up the ambience, but for the most part the streets are deserted. Tonight was quieter than usual. Several cat familiars lifted a snooty head in the air as they crossed our path, foxes nodded hello, even a few squirrels threw nuts from the rooftops. The youngsters are always rowdy around here, and I love it. The air was heavy and still, as though the town was weighed down by the heat.

A deep sense of lethargy slowly permeating my bones, making me sleepy and empty of thought.

Even after all these years, it amazes me the difference between life in a small town and that of the city. There isn't that edge, the underlying tension that makes you hunch your shoulders and move as fast as possible from one place to the next. Here, you can let your body relax, take your time, soak up the magic, and not be afraid.

Only once you are free of the confines of a large city do you realise how anxious and tense you've been for what may have been years. Small town life may have its drawbacks, as it's like everyone is watching your every move and the lack of privacy is sometimes frustrating, but there isn't that feeling of isolation, of always clenching your jaw and refusing to look people in the eye.

Our boots tapped gently on the cobbles as we made our way up the hill towards home.

The guys made jokes about me and Helen; I took them in the manner they were intended. Just us joking around because we loved each other. We all knew that she was the best thing to happen to me in a long time, and we didn't need to keep saying that, so instead they wondered out loud what she could see in me and reminded me that she was way out of my league. I reminded them that the same could be said for their partners, and none of us disagreed.

"Come on, spill the beans. How'd you get two one hundred and eighties in one night? That's incredible," said Forest.

"It was awesome," said Roger. "But you aren't usually that good. Better than most, except me, but not that good."

"Hey, I'm better at darts than you," protested Forest, but it isn't true. He's awful, and the first to admit it. It doesn't matter. We have fun, and that's the point.

"I just felt in the zone. Really focused, you know? Like when you're doing hard magic and so deep into it that everything else fades away."

"You had the power," said Roger, nodding sagely.

"The power?"

"Yeah," he said, giggling, looking like he was about to burst. "The power of love." Roger burst out laughing, then he and Forest made me suffer a full rendition of Jennifer Rush's classic being butchered by two fools who couldn't hit a note if it was pinned to a dartboard two feet away.

We laughed and joked the rest of the way home, but there was always the undercurrent of Sheila's loss. Once we were inside, we agreed that we'd visit some of the shops in the morning and see if anyone had any information, then go and check out the campsite. We'd promised Sheila we'd pick up some of her things and she'd given me the keys, so it was the perfect opportunity to snoop around and see what came up. I didn't like feeling helpless, but so far we had nothing to go on apart from the certain knowledge he'd been pushed, and a town full of potential suspects.

Thoughts ran rampant as I sipped on a coffee, knowing it was silly to be drinking it so late but needing it after the excitement of the pub. The hamper was in the kitchen, but I couldn't even face opening it. I couldn't quite come to terms with Sheila being out after what had happened. If someone I loved died, I wouldn't be down the local, drinking, and playing darts. But she wasn't me, and I shouldn't judge, as everyone handles grief differently. It was the anger that was fuelling her. And it hadn't seemed to hit her until this evening. Shock was clearly setting in, and I expected she was in a terrible state now at home. Hopefully Dad and Uncle Frank would be consoling her, and Captain would be fast asleep, snoring his head off like he always does after our Saturday night outing.

I couldn't get Helen out of my mind either. To be falling for her at a time like this felt almost insulting to Sheila's loss, and I had to stay focused and do what I could for her. But, wow, Helen was magnificent.

I drained the last of my coffee, sorted out the kitchen so it was clean for the morning, then went to bed. I had the feeling sleep would be hard to come by, especially after the coffee, but surprisingly, the moment my head hit the pillow I was fast asleep and didn't wake until the morning.

Fat Freddy's

Sunday should be a day of rest, but for the small shop owner in a town that runs on tourism, there is no such luxury. People expect to spend their money every day of the week, and as Sunday is often the last day of people's holiday before returning home, it's like they can't get rid of their money fast enough.

The cafes, restaurants, bakery, and of course the pubs, all do a roaring trade on a Sunday, and over the years the town has eased up on the restrictions we once faced, now heartily embracing a seven-day workweek. Not only does it mean the businesses earn more, mine included, but it helps to keep the younger generation local. There is always a plethora of part-time jobs for teenagers and those unable to work full-time, so it stops them having to find work in other places.

For many years, the whole of the United Kingdom had strict rules concerning Sunday opening hours, with pubs only opening for a few hours in the afternoon and all shops having to stay closed. When the laws were relaxed, Little Hope stuck to the tradition, but as tourism increased and the residents embraced, rather than tried to hide, our more magical side, then began to actively promote it, the inevitable shift occurred. Now Sunday's are like a carnival, with the high street busier than ever. Even in the winter everything is open. Tourists flock here at all times of the year, seemingly unable to get enough of our quaint town and the magnificent countryside.

And tourists need clothes. Yes, I sell plenty of the more traditional offerings classed as boho or hippy, and the number of cloaks I sell still astonishes me—when do people ever wear them?—but the shops sell well come rain or shine, as the one thing you can rely on in the UK is the unpredictable weather.

This warm, dry spell has been a real boon for everyone in town. Nobody expected it to last, believing the rain and overcast weather we usually depend on to dampen our spirits would return soon enough. The hikers have been taken by surprise, so all manner of lightweight clothing has been flying off the rails. Literally in the case of my shop and several others run by those of a magical persuasion.

After a hearty breakfast, a tradition we have on a Sunday, one more to add to the long list, we headed into town. After parking, it was a short walk to the high street where business was already roaring.

Boho chic was in full effect as people relaxed over the weekend. Local colourful characters were out enjoying the weather, some wearing so little it left nothing much at all to the imagination, while others wore thick patchwork cloaks, pointed hats, and big leather boots. The die-hard old time witches, wizards, warlocks, and others who've lived in town their whole lives often refuse to make any concessions to the weather, preferring to suffer if it means they can easily be identified as alternative. From punks to old time hippies, to those who prefer to dress smart, we have it all. It's what makes our tiny town feel like a party town. One thing we all have in common is wanting to "Stick it to The Man."

Everyone who comes here knows it's somewhere to let your hair down, not feel uncomfortable about your appearance, but rather a place to celebrate our uniqueness and yet still be part of something. A tribe. A community. And yes, a money-making endeavour too. We all have to eat.

And in our midst was a murderer.

"Stop glaring at everyone," I told Roger.

"I can't help it. One of these people could be tracking Sheila, or worse, one of us." Roger glared at an elderly couple wearing tie-dye shirts from my shop.

"Stop it, you're freaking people out."

The couple glanced back at us as they hurried past, then ducked into a shop and watched from the other side of the glass.

"I think I might be the one freaking out," blurted Roger. "I'm getting a seriously weird vibe this morning."

"You feel it too?" asked Forest.

"I think we're all feeling it," I admitted, loathe to have mentioned it but there was definitely an atmosphere. "What is it?"

Forest pulled us both aside into an alley while Kale sat at the entrance, keeping guard.

"Bran, this is your town, but you were away for a long time. You still haven't got used to everything here, and you've probably forgotten some things too, but surely you know what this is?"

Forest and Roger both nodded their heads at me, eyes eager, as if waiting for me to give the right answer.

This feeling, this intuition, hung in the air like a low cloud, and I opened myself up to it, trying to figure out what they meant. My magical radar was beeping, telling me that all was not well, that things were wrong, but what did it mean? I'd felt this way since the news of Albert's death had become common knowledge, and then it hit me.

"It's the town, isn't it? The town is worried. Is that right?"

Forest slapped me on the back as he and Roger grinned.

"He's got it," said Roger, looking much happier.

"Sure has." Forest punched me playfully on the arm. "Yes, it's the town. It senses something is off. It picks up on everyone's fears, on their nervousness, the fact this isn't good for any of us. At the moment the tourists just believe it was an accident, but the locals know what we've been up to, probably know about your visit to Calum, and what we did at the quarry, and they most likely know it all word-for-word as nothing remains secret around here longer than taking a breath, so the magical vibe is disrupted."

"And the town feels it? Look, I know I was away, but I've been back for years and I've never felt anything like this before."

"Haven't you? I bet if you think about it, then you'll realise you've always picked up on the general mood."

"Sure, I sense the general atmosphere of how everyone's feeling, you can't help it with the way everyone is here, but not the actual town."

"Bran, it's the same thing," said Roger. "The people are the town, and the town is the people. It has a heart. A mind. A soul."

With their words, it was like a whole other world opened up to me. The connection deepened, my sense of belonging, my certainty that coming home was the right move, it all heightened. That this truly was my home and I'd always belonged, just lost my way for a while.

"I feel it. The town is real!"

"Now you really are a local," laughed Forest.

"Are you crying?"

"No, just my allergies. Got something in my eye." Forest turned away and wiped at his eyes while Roger chuckled.

"We all feel it, Bran," said Roger. "Nobody ever particularly talks about it as it's just always there, you know? A connection that runs so deep you just take it for granted. Most of the time there's not even anything to feel beyond knowing you belong somewhere, that where you are is exactly where you're meant to be, but when there's a problem, or when everyone's particularly happy, then you begin to sense the change. And right now the town is most definitely anxious."

"Guess we better do our best to make Little Hope cheerful again," I told them both.

"We will," said Forest.

"Especially now Bran's finally a local."

"Hey, I've always been a local. I grew up here same as you guys."

"Yeah, but we didn't leave."

"Come on, that's unfair. It's a big world out there. Don't you ever want to see what the rest of it's like?"

"We've seen it," said Forest. "It's too big, too dirty, and too miserable. Why search for happiness when you already have it right where you are?"

"You guys should be philosophers," I chuckled.

"We're the wisest builders in town."

"You don't exactly have much competition from Marvin."

We moved back out into the sunshine, where the people looked happy but there was an undercurrent of tension that I now understood wasn't merely my mood, but the entire town's.

"I hate this place," moaned Roger as we stood outside what everyone calls Fat Freddy's but is officially named Outdoors is Lovely.

"We know," we chorused, always amused by Roger's curmudgeonly side.

"Why does he have the music so loud? Why does he have music at all? It's a shop, not a disco. And look at it, it's rammed."

We stuck our heads inside the door and watched the chaos that was Freddy's. He was his usual grinning, energetic self, dashing this way and that. Checking on customers, offering his expert opinion, and generally rushing around when he had absolutely no need to. His assistants meant he could be putting his feet up, but that isn't Freddy's style.

"Kale, are you coming in?"

"No chance. He makes me nervous." Kale sat down and turned away. Freddy is too manic for him, and always shouts, believing for some reason that the louder you talk to a dog, the better it can understand.

"Shall I wait with Kale?" asked Roger.

We dragged him inside despite his protests. Sometimes it's good to have backup, and when dealing with Freddy you definitely need it.

The moment we were in the door, a red-haired, rotund, green corduroy-wearing bundle of "fun" sporting a bow tie, a creased yellow linen shirt, and sandals almost bowled us off our feet as he dashed over, waving and talking very loudly like we hadn't seen him for years.

"The Fairfields! How wonderful." Freddy beamed as he clapped his hands together.

We said our hellos and asked about business, the usual chit-chat, before Roger blurted, "Did you meet the guy who got killed?"

Freddy's demeanour changed instantly. He lost the smile, bowed his head, and scratched at his belly. "I don't think I had the honour. Poor man. So, he definitely was killed? Why do you think he was? Was it a grisly murder?" His eyes widened in mock horror; Freddy just can't stay serious for long, bless his big heart.

"Let's just say we're looking into it," I said, casting daggers at Roger.

"So, did you meet him?" asked Roger again.

"What, me? Oh no, never set eyes on the dude. Hey, you guys want Nikes? Got the new ones with the lights on." Freddy waggled his finger and told us, "You need to get updated. Add some jazz."

"We're good for jazz, thanks." I don't know why, but that made Forest titter. "You sure you never met him? Here, take a look." I showed him the picture I'd got from Sheila, although it didn't exactly make for a memorable face.

Freddy glanced at it then shook his head, struggling to look sad. "Nope, like I said, never met the guy. I know everyone, all the locals, the regulars, and never forget a face. It's my job, see? I pride myself on remembering my

customers. And he isn't one of them. Okay, gotta go, bye."
With a wave, Freddy dove back into the melee.

From tents to footwear, walking gear to pots and pans, Freddy sells it all at high prices but nobody ever grumbles. If you appreciate his style, and to call it flamboyant is a bit of an understatement to say the least, then you're willing to pay what he asks just for the experience.

Outside, we let our ears get used to regular sound levels, then Roger said what we were all thinking. "He was acting weird. Over the top even for Freddy. And the grieving thing. What was that about? He didn't even know the guy."

"He was behaving oddly," I agreed. "Think he knows something?"

"He's just not good with stress or bad news," said Forest. "He wants the world to be a happy place, so he's never sure how to act when talking about death or anything apart from his shop. For Freddy, the world is full of rainbows and every day is a puppy party. He lives for that place and wants everyone to be dancing in the streets and singing songs. Basically, he wants life to be an eternal Fame party. He'd have us in leotards and taking drama classes if he had his way."

"Maybe, but he was quick to deny meeting Albert. He couldn't answer fast enough."

"You guys are getting carried away with suspicion," said Roger. "What, you think Freddy pushed him? Think he could even get up to the quarry?"

"He's fit, just a little overweight. He's running around all day, and have you seen his calves? They're huge. I bet he could sprint up there if he wanted to. But no, it couldn't be him." I needed to get myself under control or I'd be suspecting myself soon. Where was I at the time of the murder? I had an alibi, didn't I? I was in the shop, and must have seen loads of customers.

"Freddy wouldn't hurt a fly," said Forest. "And besides, we know we're looking for a slim man. And slim he ain't. Right, where to next?"

"We need to go to Mary's Millinery." They both groaned. This time, I agreed. The only place worse than Freddy's is Mary's. Never trust someone so obsessed with hats that they change their name so it rhymes with Millinery. We told her it didn't, but apparently it does, and she makes us agree.

Hats

"Kale, do I need to ask?" I said, smirking as he tried to edge away from Mary's.

"No, you do not. Last time I went inside I came out wearing not one, not even two, but three hats. How is that even a thing?"

"Beats me," I chuckled, remembering it well. "At least you weren't the one paying."

"I'll guard Kale," said Forest.

"And I'll guard Forest guarding Kale."

"Suit yourselves. You'll miss out on all the fun though," I winked.

"You go and enjoy yourself," said Forest, edging away with Kale and Roger before Mary saw them and dragged them inside.

Mary has one rule. If you enter her place of worship, you will leave with a hat. No question about it. She has a way of convincing even the most anti-hat person that they need one, and they had better pay up. Or else. Not that I can imagine anyone who hates hats ever going inside, as why would you?

After a deep breath, I opened the door and entered hat paradise, or hell, depending on your outlook. I appreciate a hat as much as the next man, but there are limits to my interest, or disinterest, and when it comes to magic hats, one is more than enough for me. Doesn't stop Mary trying to sell me a new wizard hat at every available opportunity, even though she knows full well that no wizard buys a hat unless the one they inherited suddenly decides to go live somewhere else. Some of them have actually upped sticks and moved to Mary's, hoping they'll get a better owner than the one they escaped.

"Bran, how wonderful!" shrieked Mary as she emerged from behind a stand lined with, no surprise here, hats. The room was full of these bespoke shelving units, with more against the walls, ensuring that everywhere you turned you were greeted with hats. Big ones, little ones, utterly massive ones, she has them all. Fedora, pork pie, trilby, boater, on and on the exhaustive list goes, and the only thing more boring than looking at the dizzying array is being lectured about them. In. Minute. Detail.

"Hi. How are you today?" I asked, trying to keep it serious and formal, when I knew I was on a losing streak before I stepped inside.

"How am I today? You sound serious? Are you on official business?" she mock-whispered, glancing around in case the hats heard.

"Official? I run a shop, same as you."

"You know what I mean. Police business? Finding out who the murderer is?" Mary adjusted her glasses, her wristful of bangles jangling, then played with the crystals hanging from her neck by leather thongs. Never one to keep still for a moment, and as jittery as ever, she then adjusted her very large, very pointy ancient hat, ran her hands down her flowing dress, and stared at her long, painted fingernails before looking up at me, somehow surprised to see me. "Bran, how nice." Mary beamed.

"How are you feeling, Mary?" I asked, knowing the answer would be the same as always.

"Oh, fine. Would you like to buy a hat? I have just the one for you. Wait here, I shan't be a mo." Mary rummaged around behind one of the units and shouted, "Did you find out who killed that poor man yet? Are you helping Calum? You seem to be solving a lot of crimes lately. It's so lovely to have you back. Are you staying, Bran?"

"Yes, I'm staying. I moved back three years ago, remember?"

"Of course I do. I know I'm rather forgetful at times, but don't treat me like I'm senile. I meant, are you definitely staying?"

"Yes, I'm not going anywhere."

"Here, try it on." Mary beamed as she held out a monstrosity in brown.

"No thank you. I have my hat, don't need another one. He wouldn't like it. You know how they get."

"I do," she sighed. "But a wizard needs a spare."

"You don't have a spare," I noted, knowing the story by heart.

"No, but only because she refuses to come off unless I'm having a shower."

Mary tapped the brim of her ever-present hat, and it shouted, "Oi!"

"That's what trying to make hats sentient does for you. And they're a bit alive already, aren't they?"

"They are. Oh, how I wish I'd never done it. But I was young and foolish and at least it gave me a lifelong interest in the blasted things." Mary laughed heartily, then turned serious as she asked, "So, if you don't want to buy a hat, what can I do for you?"

"I just wondered if you met the man that died. Albert. His wife said he purchased a new hat and coat and maybe other things. Apparently he was a keen shopper, so I wanted to check."

"Yes, he came in. I already told Calum."

"He's been here?"

"He is the local Chief. Why is that a surprise?"

"No reason. I just didn't know. So he had a photo to show you?"

"Yes. Bran, he's the police, and the poor man was murdered wasn't he?"

"Did Calum say that?"

"Not exactly, but he was asking questions and I told him straight. I sold that man a hat, but it wasn't the right one, and he was very rude. Didn't even smile."

"What happened?" I could only imagine how well Mary's opinion on his choice of hat went down with Albert.

"He picked a terrible shape, and the shade was all wrong. I offered to help him choose, but he wouldn't hear of it. He made his purchase then went off in a huff. Horrid man." Mary put a hand to her mouth, eyes wide, and blurted, "But I didn't kill him. He was just rude, but I know I shouldn't speak ill of the dead."

"It's fine," I reassured her. "I met him too, and he wasn't the nicest guy. We don't have to like everyone, even if they're dead."

"Oh, good, because there are lots of dead people that I dislike."

"Anything else happen that you can think of? Did he say where he was going? What else he'd bought?"

"He said he had bought a lightweight jacket but I didn't ask where, and he said he wasn't going to buy anything else, but I know his type. He was lying."

"Lying? What makes you think that?"

"He looked shifty."

"How so?"

"It's all in the eyes. He was shifty."

The door opened and a woman entered, eyes wide with delight when she took in Mary's stock. They always react in one of two ways. They get a dreamy, faraway look in their eyes as they can't believe they've finally found hat heaven, or they're utterly horrified and turn straight back around and hurry out before Mary gets her red-painted claws into them.

"Thanks. See you soon, Mary. I'll let you deal with your customer."

I hurried out as Mary called after me, "But you didn't buy a hat!"

I got away with it this time, but knew if I ever stepped foot inside again I'd be buying two or never hear the end of it.

The gang was hiding around the corner, so I joined them and took several deep breaths to recover.

"Anything?" asked Forest.

"He bought a hat. She said he was rude and grumpy and bought the wrong one, but nothing else. Oh, and he bought a jacket somewhere, but said that was all he was buying."

"So it's a dead end?"

"It all helps give us an idea of Albert's activities. But pretty much a dead end, yes."

"How did Mary seem?" asked Roger. "Think she's going senile?"

"The same as usual. Bit forgetful at first, and scatty as always, but she's doing well. I think every witch of fifty and over in this town is that way. Same for wizards. The older they get, the less they take notice of the everyday. Get more stuck in their ways."

"Bran," laughed Forest, "it isn't just the over fifties. And that's not so far away for any of us now. All adults in Little Hope can be forgetful and seem odd. It's the magic. This energy flying about, the elders casting spells like they're going out of fashion, the magic permeating everything the same way it has for so many generations, it makes for an odd place with even odder people."

"Maybe you're right. She just seemed more distracted than usual."

"She's busy. This heatwave means she's making a fortune. Mary has always prided herself on giving every customer her individual attention. She can't do that when there are so many of them. Oh, and she is as fruity as a Christmas pudding."

"Hey, I thought you said she was doing fine."

"She is, but she's still one crazy old witch. Her family have always been rather obsessive. It's in the blood. Makes it hard work to deal with them sometimes."

"That hat scares me," said Kale. "It looks at me."

"It hasn't got eyes," I told him, smiling as I ruffled his head. The connection between us deepened at my touch, same as always, and my spirits soared as our love sang out between us. Private, and so deep sometimes it physically hurts.

"Doesn't mean it isn't looking at me. And it knows things." Kale shuddered.

"What things?"

"Just things. Did you ask it any questions?"

"I am not about to start asking every sentient inanimate object questions about Albert. We'll be here for weeks if I do."

"Just an idea. Can you straighten my neckerchief, I think it's gone wonky."

"You look great, same as always." Regardless, I shifted the red and white bandana so it was perfectly aligned, then stood back and asked, "Better?"

"Much." Kale stood, stretched out his large, slender frame, then turned to us, head cocked to one side. "Can we go somewhere with more grass and less cobbles? I'll need a poo soon. Did you bring the bags?"

"Don't I always?" I sighed. There is one massive drawback to sharing your world with one of the largest breeds, and it's a very smelly one. At times like this I wish a chihuahua had singled me out to be my familiar. "Can you hold it for a while?"

"Of course," said Kale, insulted.

I told the guys what the plan was as they zone out now when Kale and I are talking, then we continued through town questioning the few remaining shop owners. Nobody recalled selling him a coat, or anything else.

There was just one more stop to be made, then we'd head off to the campsite and get Sheila's things.

Goth Time

"Stop staring at your sign like you want to eat it," chided Forest, doing his brotherly thing and punching my arm. I know he means well when he does it, but I've got a dent because he loves me so much.

"I just think it's cool. Dad's got a real talent for sign-writing, hasn't he?"

"More like carving. Yeah, it looks terrific. Dad's an expert with a chisel, and you actually got him interested in woodworking again because of this sign. Now he's done half the ones in town."

"And the place looks better for it. Makes it more cohesive. A proper style."

We looked up the street at the various shops, many of which did now have a hand-carved piece of what Dad likes to call his chipping, and the shop owners call art.

"You did well," said Forest, draping an arm over my shoulder. "I knew you'd make this place a success."

"Really? You've never said that before."

Forest shrugged. "We're men approaching middle age. We don't talk about our feelings, we talk about plasterboard and concrete mix ratios. We go to the pub and make fun of each other, or complain about old people, mostly our parents and Captain. But I am proud of you."

"And I'm proud of you too. All of you." I grinned at Roger and Kale who both nodded.

"I helped with the sign too," said Kale, put out that he hadn't been mentioned.

"Yes, you did," I told him, smiling at the paw print and wizard hat motif on the sign.

"It's good we're together again," said Roger. "It's been a tough few years for everyone, but we pull through, stick together, and try to fend off Captain's staff."

We laughed at the mention of Captain. We love him, but he does need to control his staff better.

"Think we're doing the right thing here?" I asked them. "Are we messing things up for Calum? Are we nothing more than busybodies?"

"Look, Bran, we know you have this thing with Calum, but let's be honest here. He's been going through the motions ever since Emily died. It's really hard on him, and you, but he has a job to do and for years he wasn't doing it. Even now he's not acting how he used to, and he dismissed this as an accident without looking into it properly." Forest nodded to Roger.

"He's right," said Roger. "Calum may be asking around now, but only because we got involved. Sheila asked for our help, so we're doing what we can. There's no point pretending we're detectives, but we do alright, and have uncovered more than Calum has. Sure, he's annoyed with you, but that's tough. We know he's a broken man, and it's a terrible thing, but we can't let that stop us doing what we feel is right. Helping friends, old or brand new like Sheila, is more important than his feelings right now, so let's just get on with this thing and give Sheila closure. Okay?"

"Okay," I agreed. "Thanks. I needed that pep talk. I'll just check on the youngster then we can go to the campsite. Hazel Hollow will be bursting at the seams, I expect, but we might find answers there." I pushed open the door, the bell rang, and I entered what has been, and always will be, my sanctuary. Bran's Dream.

"Hey Bran." Myrtle waved cheerily from across the room, where she was showing a customer the mild potions I'd brewed up and explaining how they worked. She was itching to learn, but I wasn't the one to teach her, and it would be my hide if I even tried. The maternal side of her family is in charge of that, and much else in her life, right until the moment she dies, and most likely afterwards too. There are some traditions you do not meddle with, not if you value your current human form and the ability to walk down the street without everyone muttering.

"How have you been on your own?" I asked, looking around nervously in case the place had gone to rack and ruin in a morning. "Were you okay yesterday? I didn't come to see you. I normally do."

"Fine. No problems. And I have worked alone before. Every Sunday in fact. You don't have to keep coming in to check on me."

"I know, but I can't help it."

Myrtle served the customer and they left after a brief chat.

"You fret too much," said Grenadine as I wandered around the shop like I was a fascist shop inspector with a badge, here to judge sixteen-year-olds trying to earn their money rather than rely on their parents. Maybe take her in for questioning, see if she'd break and admit to not coping and just pretending she was a capable teenager able to open and close tills and count.

"I know," I told the smug spider as she zipped along a web then curled her legs in and closed her eyes. Then, seemingly changing her mind, Grenadine's eyes snapped open, she launched at me, landed on my shoulder, and whispered, "Did you catch the killer? I forgot all about it, but I don't want to get squished. Was it a dark mage? Maybe a vampire? Ugh, they give me the creeps." Grenadine shuddered, I tried not to, as she takes it personally if you act scared of her, then she jumped back onto her web and glared at me with all eight eyes, waiting for an answer.

"I'll let you know the moment I find out, but don't you worry, we won't let anything happen to you."

With a nod, she pulled her legs in and settled once more.

"Hey, I heard you did really well at the darts yesterday. Well done." Myrtle tidied behind the counter while we spoke, efficient and seemingly happy in her work. She's the only one who can understand Grenadine apart from me, which makes me certain she's destined for tremendous things.

"Thanks. I was in the zone. You need anything? Mum okay? The gnomes behaving? Any trouble?"

"Bran, everything's fine. Standin' has been a bit of a pain, but nothing new there, right?"

"He gets like that sometimes. Give him an important job to do like arranging the joss sticks by length and he'll cheer right up."

We turned to watch him chatting away angrily at us, pointing to the already neat rows of incense sticks.

"He's so funny," chuckled Myrtle, smiling widely. She caught herself being cheerful and tried to look fed up, but it just isn't in her nature. She adores all things goth, or maybe they call it emo now, and prefers to wear dark vests, heavy eye-liner, and even black lipstick. She always wears her Doc Martens and holey tights with a black skirt, but she can't look grumpy for more than a few seconds.

"So, you're okay in here alone then?"

"Bran, I keep telling you, I got this. I've been working here for months now. You enjoy your time off. I like it. You pay well, better than everyone else, the shop's warm, I get to meet some cool people, and it gets mum and dad off my back about money. I like having the independence, and it means I have cash to spend on what I want. It's all cool. Plus, me and Grenadine have a right laugh. She's such a fun gal."

"Sorry, I know you can handle it. You're doing great and I'm glad you're here to help out. Should I pop in before closing time?"

"You don't have to. I've got my own keys and have I ever not locked up? No, I haven't. Go hang with your brother and cousin. I'll be fine."

Knowing she was right, and amazed as always at how mature she was for such a young girl, I left her to it and tried not to stop to rearrange anything on my way out.

"It's like she's a forty-year-old in a teenager's body," I told the others outside.

"You worry too much," said Roger. "Myrtle's a great girl. Smart, patient, always lively, and she'll make a great witch in a few years. If her folks don't mess things up."

We all knew Myrtle's story, that it wasn't the best of a home life for her and her brother, but she was coping admirably, they both did well in school, and with this job Myrtle made it easier for her parents to get by. Money is tight for them. Not everyone's story in Little Hope is one of prosperity, but the youngsters are great kids, even if the parents are what the locals like to call a little rough around the edges. If they're being kind.

Meaning, her folks are proper magic users of the old tradition. So, naturally, they live in squalor in the woods in a rundown shack and stick to the ways practised for generations by all our ancestors. They love a good cackle, are big on warts and black cats, prefer to catch and eat squirrels rather than buy meat from the butcher's, and see jobs as something of a crime against witches and wizards, believing they have better things to do with their time. It isn't a unique situation. Dotted around the area are scores of others living very similar lives. It's just another part of the rich tapestry of Little Hope that makes it unique and a mecca for those searching for a different way to live.

But they don't seem to mind Myrtle working for me, and it gives her a different perspective on the world, so I'm happy to help out. I had a few cross words with her parents when she first began, but I soon put their minds at ease, promising I would look after her and it wouldn't interfere with either school or her magic training. Since then, things have settled down—they never come into the shop and I steer clear of them.

A Box of Confusion

At the gate to the campsite, Landrie, the no-nonsense woman who runs it, stood with her feet planted wide, her arms folded across her ample chest, and her long, straight hair plastered to her rosy cheeks.

"She doesn't look happy," noted Roger.

"She looks ready to blow," agreed Forest.

"What she needs is a hat. But I doubt she's in the mood for a shopping trip." I pulled up in the car park beside the large cabin Landrie uses to book people in and out and where she spends more time than she'd like. She comes from a long line of farmers, and looks the part down to her dirty jeans, her practical boots, ruddy cheeks, and flowing auburn hair she likes to remind people is the colour of a rusty tractor. Today she looked like she'd been dragged through a hedge backwards, not that I was about to mention that.

"Hey," I called, waving.

Landrie glanced our way as the guys called hello, scowling at the sound of vehicles crunching across the gravel, a constant stream of people coming and going.

"What is wrong with all these people?" she snapped, glaring at them as they entered or left the cabin where her staff were sorting the bookings.

"Having some problems?" I asked.

"Nobody seems able to tell the time. Either they're turning up early, or leaving late, or coming a day before they should and hoping I can squeeze them in. Sure, we have the room, we've got acres to spare, but it's the admin. Ugh, it's driving me crazy. And this heat! I want snow, not sun." Landrie peeled a handful of hair from her cheek and dabbed at her neck with a rag.

Kale sauntered over and rubbed his head against her jeans; he has a real thing for Landrie. I think it's the smell of the animals.

"Hey buddy," she said, stroking him, her spirits visibly lifting. If Landrie had her way she'd spend her days riding horses, wandering fields of sheep with her dogs, and communing with cows whilst honing her spells, but farming doesn't pay like it should, and never has.

"At least you're busy," said Roger with a smile, mostly ignoring the rant as we all knew she loved when it was busy and she had something to complain about. It meant she could spend more on horses.

"Don't get smart with me, Roger, or I'll bend you over my knee." She laughed freely, deep and hearty, and everyone relaxed. "Hear you have Sheila at the madhouse. How's that working out for you?"

"Great for us, as we're leaving our dads and Captain to look after her," I said. "We promised we'd collect some things for her. What do you think happened? Anything you can do to help?"

Landrie shrugged. "It's a mystery. Calum was over, giving me the third degree like it's all my fault. I told him the same as I'll tell you. I have no idea what happened. Sheila and her husband turned up, then when their spot was available they parked and set up for their holiday. She seemed nice, him not so much."

"Anything out of the ordinary happen around the time they arrived or after? Anyone acting strangely?"

Landrie studied me for a long time, then asked, "Are you seriously asking if anyone around here acts strangely? If they didn't, that would be more concerning. Look at it. Look at them. Most of these people are oddballs."

We watched the display of vehicles, the people coming and going, and, of course, she was right.

"So nothing that has you worried?"

"It all worries me. I can't get a minute's peace. I wish I could help you guys out. That poor woman must be losing her mind, but there's nothing I can think of. Just lots of tourists. And let's be honest, everyone just comes and goes as they please. We book them in and out, but we miss plenty when they leave. And if they're walking they do what they like. Sorry, I have to go." Landrie rushed off to the cabin where we heard raised voices complaining about not being allowed to book in a day early.

"Look how busy this place is," said Roger. "It's not normally like this, is it?"

"You haven't been here for a while. It gets absolutely rammed in the summer. And the weather this year means it's bound to be even busier. Let's just find Sheila's van and get her some things."

We drove along the gravel road running the length of the campsite. Further into the fields, it was grass only, but for the electric hook-up points the road ensured heavy vehicles didn't chew up the ground and trash the place.

"There it is," said Forest, pointing to my right.

"It looks like it, but that's not the right registration," I said, slowing.

"And there's another one over there. What gives with all these identical Volkswagen vans?" said Roger.

"It's a mini revolution. After all that's gone on in the world recently, everyone's realised that it's actually nice to holiday in your own country. And campervans are the best way to do it. There's a booming trade in converting all kinds of vans, and they're pretty cool now. It's cheaper than faffing about going to the other side of the world, you can get home without the risk of being stuck in an airport or a hotel abroad for weeks, and you can eat what you want. That's why there are so many more people in Wailing Wood too. We've got more tourists than ever. You guys know that."

"There have been loads more out-of-towners getting their holiday homes done up," agreed Forest, rubbing his hands together. "We've been busier than ever."

"Sure have," said Roger. "Long may it last. But only as long as they don't stop locals being able to buy their own homes."

"It's definitely a problem for some towns," I agreed, keeping an eye out for Sheila's van. "But there aren't that many around here. Just enough to keep you guys busy."

"That's the way we like it," said Forest. "There, is that it?" He pointed at another Volkswagen.

"Wrong curtains. Red, remember."

"Then it must be that one." Forest nodded to a bay on our right. I checked the registration and it matched. This was Sheila's.

"We found it. Finally." This place is nuts though. Look how tightly they're crammed in. You can hardly move."

I parked alongside the camper at a right angle as there was no space to parallel park. The vehicles either side were monstrosities, more like true homes on wheels than something you'd go on holiday in. Motorhomes for large families, and more than likely permanent abodes. How do people even drive these things around small towns and villages? You'd need a heavy goods licence to drive one, for a start.

The place was buzzing. People were everywhere, and my guess was that it didn't calm down much in the night. Groups of youngsters were sitting around tents and gazebos nursing hangovers in the best way they could think of—they were already on the beer. Other visitors were sorting out tents and arranging chairs, and most of those with campervans were sitting outside under extendable awnings, enjoying the fresh morning air.

Sheila's much more modest van was wedged between the two beasts, with most of the available space taken up by fold-out picnic benches and strings of washing. You ran the risk of tripping over or getting decapitated. Our new house guest was definitely safer with us. If the murderer didn't get her, then the washing definitely would.

We dodged the knickers, the breathable walking vests and shirts, tried not to bang a shin on the chairs, tables, and benches, and slid alongside Sheila's van. I unlocked the door with the key she'd given me and we all squeezed inside.

"Wow, this is nice," whistled Forest. "Look, it even has a proper oven." Forest plonked himself down in the seating area arranged around a table that could be folded up and slid into the panelling, Roger eased in beside him, and I went to the back and sat on a bench that apparently became a double bed.

"I could use one of these," I pined.

"What for? You haven't been anywhere since you moved back. You don't even take a day off. You work way too hard."

"I have Saturday afternoons off now, and never work Sundays. See, I'm here, aren't I?"

"You usually end up going back to the shop on Saturdays even though you have the youngster working there now. But that's only recently. Before that you always worked Saturdays," said Roger.

"And now you don't, you come and work with us. Same on Sundays if we have a rush job," said Forest.

"And if you aren't with us, you're back at the shop sorting out stock or making dream catchers, or going for walks. And you spend way too much time with the blackbirds."

"Guys, can you hear yourselves? Going for a walk is taking a day off. And you both work harder and for longer hours than I do. What's your problem with blackbirds? They're the best birds, and if I'm nice they save feathers for the dream catchers."

"It's different," said Forest. "We have holidays. We book off a week here, a fortnight there, and take it easy. Recuperate. Chill out. You're always busy. You don't just sit and relax."

"I relax. I read, I walk, I watch TV, I hang with you guys. I take Kale out twice a day."

"You haven't today," he said as he stepped into the van then sniffed. "Smells strange in here. Like old carpet."

"It's not the newest of vans. Sheila's husband bought it for a good price apparently as it needed updating, but he didn't want to spend the money. I think they both underestimated how expensive it would be to get it renovated. I like it."

Kale came over to me and I smoothed his head as he rested it on the bench. There was almost no room to move now he was here, and sorting through the cupboards to find Sheila's stuff would be hard with us jammed in.

"Why don't you go keep watch outside?" I suggested.

"For what?"

"Anybody, I guess. Someone's out to get Sheila, remember? We need to look after her and maybe they'll come looking here. See if anyone looks suspicious."

"Fine, but I know this is just your way of saying I'm fat," huffed Kale.

"You aren't fat! You're too skinny if anything."

"Oh, so now I'm skinny? Way to boost a guy's confidence."

"No, what I meant is you aren't fat. You're perfect." I rubbed his head and smiled.

Kale harrumphed, then barged his way out, making sure to bang into everything as he said, "Oh, so sorry. Must be because my body's suddenly the wrong shape. Bits of me are fat, and others are tiny."

I rolled my eyes as he jumped out.

"What was that all about?" asked Roger.

"I think he's feeling left out. He likes to help."

"He'll get over it. Right, can we grab her gear and get out of here? I don't know what the smell is in here, but I don't like it." Forest screwed up his nose, then heaved himself out of the bench seat.

"Definitely a bit whiffy. It seems familiar." I opened a cupboard to see if it contained Sheila's clothes and stepped back, gagging.

"What the hell is that?" croaked Roger.

"Close the door," coughed Forest.

I slammed the cupboard shut and took a step back. I would have taken two, but there was no room.

We eyed each other then laughed. "I really wish we didn't have such a good sense of smell. It's a real pain at times."

"Just one of the perks of being a Fairfield," said Forest, wiping his eyes.

"I knew I recognised the smell. It's like concentrated Snodgrass. Why does anyone ever even enter his gross shoe shop?"

"People like it because it's traditional, I guess." I shrugged. "Albert must have been there and bought shoes then stuffed them in the cupboard. Damn, but it stinks." I opened the door and peered at the shoe box.

"What are you doing?" screamed Roger. "Close it. I don't want Snodgrass stink all over me."

"It's just shoes," I laughed, not really sure why, but staring at the box like it had answers. "Maybe Sheila bought them? Do you think?"

"Maybe. But we aren't taking them with us. Bran, what are you doing?"

"I'm not sure," I replied honestly, picking up the box and shaking it. The dull thud of footwear banging against cheap cardboard somehow reassured me.

"You'll never get that smell off your hands," warned Roger. "I thought it was the carpet in here, but no, it's the smell of Snodgrass' foul carpet and the stink of cabbage that gets stuck to everything in his gross shop. Why won't he clean up his act?"

"Some people, people like Albert, I'm guessing, prefer the old-fashioned kind of shoe shop. Don't you remember when we were young? Everyone went there. It was how you expected the place to be. Thin carpet, weird musty smell of wet cardboard, grumpy old guy who shoved your feet into shoes with that plastic thing he slid over your heel. Albert's from a different generation. He wouldn't appreciate Freddy's style." I shook the box once more then couldn't resist taking a peek. It was a pair of walking boots.

"Satisfied now?" asked Forest, looking at me strangely.

"I think so. Come on, let's get Sheila's things and take off." I opened the window to let more fresh air in, then we banged cupboard doors and searched in nooks and crannies until we figured we had enough for a day or two.

I washed my hands until the smell was mostly gone, then dried them on a towel and arranged it neatly on the little rail. The window slid closed with a satisfying *clunk*. Can't beat German engineering.

Outside, we breathed deeply and I closed the door on Sheila's tiny little home on wheels.

We turned as Kale growled.

"What is it?" I asked.

"A man's heading straight for us."

"Is he coming to do harm?"

"No, more confused than anything. And a bit annoyed. Not dangerous. At least, I don't think so."

"Be nice," I told Kale, then nudged the guys.

We watched as a man in his twenties sauntered over to us, looking hot and bothered even though he only wore frayed shorts, sandals, and was shirtless.

"Hey," he said, waving and smiling.

We moved out into the open and next to Kale who watched him with deep focus.

"Hi. Nice day," I offered.

"Yeah, bit hot though. I've been traipsing around all over, and keep getting the wrong place. This is it though. I recognise the grass."

"The grass?"

"Yeah," he chuckled, rubbing at his mop of bleached blond hair. "It's where we had a fire the other day. Burnt the grass, see?" He pointed at a charred spot of ground and laughed. "Bit of a wild night."

"So you've been looking for this pitch?"

"Yeah. Um, look, this might sound weird, and it certainly has to the three other vans just like this one I've already been to. Everyone thought I was mad, but I'm not, promise."

"Sorry, you lost me there," I said, confused.

"That's what they all said. But this is the right place so it must be you guys. This your VW?"

"No, it's a friend of ours. She's staying with us for a while. She just lost her husband."

"Damn, man, that sucks. How did he die?"

"He fell off a cliff," said Roger.

"Oh, that dude? We heard about him. Didn't know it was someone staying here. Weird coincidence."

"What is?"

"Okay, look, I better explain before you think I'm a nutter. Like I said, I've been trying to find this campervan. I kept going to the wrong spot, but figured they might have moved, but now I know I'm at the right place."

"You've still lost me," I admitted.

"We were camping here. The other day. We spent a night to get charged up, as it's nice having a little luxury now and then, then we went to Wailing Wood the next day. We do it every year. Saves money, and it's so cool there. I can't get enough of them complaining trees. So awesome." He smiled, clearly rather embarrassed.

"Of course. A lot of people do it," I said.

"Yeah, right. Well, here's the thing, as we were leaving, a campervan, this one," he pointed at Sheila's van, "was driving past us. They took the spot just as we left. Me and the missus had a laugh about it. I mean, it was just one of those weird coincidences. But it made us laugh."

"There are a few of them around now," I agreed. "But yes, still quite a coincidence. But I'm still not getting why you were looking for it."

"This is going to sound mad as a wart with a frog on it, but I don't suppose you know if the owners are missing some shoes, do you?"

"Shoes?"

"Yeah. Um, walking boots. Go on your feet." The man tugged nervously at his shorts, almost as dark as his deep tan, then pointed at his own feet like we didn't understand. "I was looking for something yesterday and I opened a cupboard and there was this weird smell. Really strong. Like old carpet or cabbage or something. It was this." He pulled out a box from the bag he was carrying and showed us. "It's boots," he said, then laughed. "Sorry, stating the obvious here. I found the box and it was just super weird. We couldn't figure it out. Then something clicked, and I thought, hey, I bet someone mistook our camper for their own. We never lock it, there's nothing worth nicking inside, so we figured maybe someone came in and put the box in our cupboard thinking it was their cupboard. You get what I'm saying?"

"I understand what you think, but I still don't get why you'd think that?" I told him.

"Figured maybe the owners thought it was their van and really it was ours. That maybe there was some confusion and they stashed the box not realising."

"But you said you saw this van come and take your spot," said Forest. "Why would they think it was their van when they hadn't even been here yet?"

"People park up, waiting for a spot, right? They get given their pitch but often have to wait around for hours. I dunno, I thought maybe the owners, or one of them or something had come back and thought their wife or husband or whatever had moved their van and that's how it ended up in ours. Am I way off track here?" he asked, looking flustered and beyond confused.

"Honestly, I'm not sure," I said. "Maybe Sheila's husband could have come back and put the shoes in the wrong van, but we've just been in there and there's a box of shoes in a cupboard from the same shop."

"Whoa, that is beyond weird. Nobody buys two pairs of shoes at different times on the same day, so I guess I got this all messed up. What do I do now? I hate to think of someone missing their new boots, but this box stinks. What should I do?"

"Maybe keep hold of it and see if anyone asks." I shrugged, unsure what to tell him.

"I think your best bet is to tell the campsite owner. Landrie's a nice woman when she isn't running around getting stressed. She can ask around. But you were only here for a day, right?" asked Roger.

"Yeah, now we're down the hill."

"Have you asked there?"

"I have, and nobody is missing a pair of small boots. What do you reckon, someone stole them or something and just put them in our cupboard?"

"Why would they do that?" I asked.

"Mate, I have absolutely no idea," he admitted. "I'm pretty sure I just made a fool of myself and I've got all confused. I just thought maybe because we had the same camper that things got mixed up. But now that makes no sense. You're right, we were gone before they got here, so how could they have put the shoes in our van? Sorry, I think I need to go have a lie down. Maybe I'll just hand the shoes in at reception and be done with it. If anyone asks, that's where they'll be."

He nodded to us then turned to leave.

"Oh, what size were they?" I asked.

"Size? Why?"

"I'm not sure. Just wondered," I admitted.

"They were seven and a half. Weird size, eh? They're men's, but that's pretty small." He swung the bag over his shoulder and wandered off slowly, looking dejected.

"He really wants to find the owner of those boots," laughed Roger.

"Sure does," I agreed. "Bit weird that both vans have ones from the same shop. Why would someone put them in his van?"

"Like he said, they just got mixed up. There are quite a few of them and if you don't remember where you parked, it's an easy mistake to make. They all look the same inside."

"You'd notice the moment you opened the door that it wasn't your van. Everyone has their own touch to make things more personal," said Forest. "You don't make a mistake like that."

"But somebody did," I said. "Or did they?"

"Well, yeah, they did," said Roger. "That poor guy just told us so. Someone put a box of Snodgrass junk in his vehicle. It's nice of him to try to return them, but I don't think he was the sharpest tool in the box."

"He might have just found them when he was drunk and doesn't even remember," suggested Forest. "And he's flaky. Seems like a stoner to me. Probably got high and forgot he even bought them."

"Nah, just a daft mistake," said Roger. "I bet there's another van just like his and Sheila's down in the woods and they just got confused. He couldn't have bought them himself as they weren't his size."

"Or could he?" I asked.

"Will you stop saying that!" snapped Forest. "It's really annoying."

"Or is it?" I asked, smiling.

"Yes!" they both shouted.

With Sheila's overnight bag safely stowed, we crawled out of the campsite, and just in time by the seems of it. Scores of vehicles were waiting in the car park to be allocated spaces, and judging by the number of utterly lost looking visitors wandering about, it seemed like Landrie had gone missing and wasn't sorting out the mess.

We spied the young lad with his box standing outside the checking-in cabin looking utterly confounded. Poor man just wanted to do the right thing. He shrugged, and wandered off back to the woods, still carrying the bag with the box inside.

"Wait!" shouted Kale.

I slammed on the brakes and gasped, "What's wrong?"

"I forgot to have my poo. I need to go. Now!"

Muttering, I dove out of the car, let Kale run off into the trees, and grabbed a handful of poo bags.

"You get to have all the fun," joked Roger.

I grunted at him then went to clean up after Kale. Landrie would string me up by things I cherished if she discovered I'd left a mess anywhere where her guests might be wandering about. She isn't averse to using her deep knowledge of the natural world to cause all kinds of problems for anyone who gets in her way. She's a very adept maker of unique and particularly nasty spells based around fungal growth, and I've heard enough stories to know never to cross her.

As usual, Kale's poo stop took an age. He insisted on marking all available trees, then needed to have a run around, and I only convinced him to return after I promised him some treats. Sometimes it's easy to forget that he is, at heart, a dog, and more than anything just wants to play.

Cabbage and Shoes

The town was particularly busy, and I was tempted to stop in at the shop but forced myself not to. The guys snorted as I told them, making fun of me for obsessing about the business. It wasn't that I was concerned about the money as such, although it was nice the place was doing so well, it was more that I felt proud of myself for having got it up and running and had a focus.

Something to occupy my time, keep me on my toes, and a challenge, albeit one that consists of counting joss sticks and making dream catchers for the most part. I also enjoy the magic side of the business, which has come as a surprise. I love reading Tarot, find deep satisfaction in small-scale spells and giving advice when asked for, and letting the magic within bubble to the surface for a while.

Was it the power? Maybe. But it goes deeper than that. I relish finally being able to be who I truly am. No more hiding, pretending to be something I'm not. I am not like other people. We are different. My family is different. For the first time in my life, I embraced that when I came home. I'm not afraid to admit it to myself or others. It's truly liberating to no longer care what other people think.

"I think we should go and talk to Snodgrass now," I told the others.

Kale whined from the back seat. So did Forest and Roger.

"Do we have to?" whined Forest.

"I hate it in there. And he's so depressing," whined Roger.

See, told you they whined.

"Can I wait outside?" asked Kale.

"No, you can come in. You might pick up on something."

"You talking to me?" asked Roger.

"No, Kale."

It's an endless source of confusion. I prefer to talk to Kale out loud, but I'm not always certain that I do, and I can never keep track of if he's talking telepathically to me or barking so others at least hear him.

"Why are we going in there?" asked Forest. "This about the shoes? Leave it to the kid. He'll hand them in and that's the end of it."

"You know we have to follow this up. Stop acting like there's a choice. Something's bugging me about it. And we checked the other shops earlier, in case anyone knew anything. We should have gone to Snodgrass' too."

"He's got one of his feelings," sang Forest, excited.

"Bran's on the case," squealed Roger, clapping his hands.

"Guys, calm down. You're acting like excited children going to the park," I laughed.

"We love it when you get your wizard senses tingling. What do you reckon then?"

"I have no idea. But this boot business is bugging me. Why would anyone put their purchase in someone else's camper? Did Albert buy two pairs and hide one?"

"But it's nothing to do with the case," protested Forest. "It's just a screwup."

"Or is it?" I asked.

"Yes!" they both shouted.

We laughed as I parked. After a short walk through the busy streets, we stood outside Snodgrass Shoes and milled about, none of us wanting to enter.

"Maybe this wasn't such a good idea," I mused. "It's just a pair of smelly boots. Not very nice ones either."

"Yes, but it's a mystery, right? And we know you won't rest until you figure it out. It'll bug you until you do."

I laughed. "You know me too well. Okay, Kale, lead the way."

Kale turned and glared. He cocked his head to the side and merely waited. "Fine, I'll go first, but you're all coming in."

Looking like they were being sent to the headmaster's office, they hung their heads but I knew they would always back me up.

The assault on the nasal passages was almost overwhelming. Damp carpet, old shoes, smelly socks, and a distinct aroma of cheese and tuna. Add some boiled cabbage into that and you have a recipe for Snodgrass. We gagged as we spread out at the front of the shop, cursing our keen sense of smell. Kale whimpered from the door, snorting fresh air from the crack in the warped frame.

Surprisingly, and it's always a shock, the shop wasn't empty. It wasn't exactly a party, nobody else in here was under fifty, but Snodgrass somehow always seems to have customers. Maybe it's a declining sense of smell that ensnares the somewhat older generation, or maybe a wistful reminiscence of shops from a bygone era, or maybe the reassuringly reasonable price tags on the various shoes, walking boots, and unfashionable trainers are the true lure. Or the choice offered. Snodgrass sells what he calls timeless classics, and most others call old-fashioned footwear. Captain loves the place, but despises the man so much he refuses to enter. Even our dads have been known to put up with Snodgrass to buy a pair of what they think of as cool and modern boots but are far from it.

We waited patiently, which is an utter lie. The ghastly fumes were playing havoc with our sinuses and my eyes were stinging, but eventually the customers were served, or left empty-handed, leaving just a few browsers.

"No dogs," warned Snodgrass, marching over. "I don't want that beast stinking out my shop."

My mouth opened and closed in mute astonishment, but I nodded, then opened the door. Kale bolted, laughing as he did so.

"Can we have a quick word?" I asked, putting on my polite voice.

"What's wrong with you? What's wrong with him?" he asked Forest, shaking his head. "Why does he sound like he's pretending to be Australian?"

"What? I'm not. I was being polite."

"Stop it! It's making me want to light the barbecue. What do you want? Come to tell me you're closing down Fat Freddy's, are you?" he asked hopefully.

"Not exactly."

"Then what? I'm busy."

"Did you sell a pair of boots to someone a few days ago? In fact, did you sell a few pairs to a few people?" asked Forest.

"What are you talking about? Of course I did. I run a shoe shop. Are you losing your marbles? Have you gone soft in the head?" Snodgrass rapped his knuckles on Forest's forehead and shouted, "Hello, anyone in there?"

Forest was halfway through a spell that would see Snodgrass cowering in a cupboard for the foreseeable future. A dark spell designed to give the recipient a phobia. I knew he'd use footwear as his chosen weapon before I nudged him and he reluctantly let it dissipate.

"You know about the murder, yes?"

"Of course. What? Wait! Murder?" Snodgrass' eyes narrowed. He brushed the dried skin flakes off his shoulder as he thought it through. He's always looking for an angle and was no doubt wondering how this could benefit him.

"I meant death. The man who fell from the quarry ridge. We spoke about it the other day."

"Yes, what about it?" He looked nervous, wringing his hands as his red-rimmed eyes glanced around the shop. "Calum didn't say it was a murder. He just asked if I met the man who died."

"Did you sell him a pair of boots?"

"Don't you go trying to insinuate that it was my boots that made him fall. And anyway," he crowed, "you just said it was a murder, so it couldn't have been the boots."

"I wasn't suggesting your boots had anything to do with it. But you did sell him a pair?"

"Maybe I did, maybe I didn't," he growled.

"If you don't give us some straight answers, I swear I'll make you so terrified of any and all footwear that you'll be a gibbering wreck by the end of the day," warned Forest.

"Fine, fine, yes, I sold him a pair of boots. Nice ones, real quality, not the kind that would make you fall off a cliff. Or get pushed. And besides, I've already told this to Police Chief Swift. What business is it of yours?"

"What did Calum say?"

"None of your business! I'm not about to divulge confidential information to the likes of you."

"Come on, Snodgrass," laughed Roger, "he wouldn't share any information with you. We just wondered what kind of thing he was asking."

"Just ask your questions and leave. I'm a busy man." Snodgrass puffed out his chest and indicated the shop, like he didn't have a moment to spare. His young assistant was helping someone into a horrendous pair of fake leather slip-ons. Nobody else looked in need of assistance.

"So, you sold a pair of boots to Albert, the dead man?" I asked.

"Yes. I already told you."

"And have you sold any to anyone else?"

"I just said I have. Quite a few pairs. It's a busy time. Although it would be busier if you sorted out Fat Freddy."

"I'll have a word with Captain." I wouldn't.

"Anyone act strange? Any odd purchases?"

"How'd you mean?"

"I don't know. Just wondered if anyone has been acting strange."

"Everyone in this town is strange. If they aren't turning things into toads, then they're wishing they were. And if you don't get to the point, I'll turn the lot of you into

a bunch of idiots. Oh no, I can't, because you already are."
He cackled at his own joke. Nobody else even smirked.

"Did you sell a size seven and a half to anyone? Did it
seem like an odd purchase?"

"How did you know?" he gasped. "I did. A man came
in and just picked up one of the boxes from over there." He
pointed at a stack of old stock piled up with a sale sign above
it. "He just grabbed a box and brought it to the till. The
fellow was in a terrible hurry. I asked him if he was sure the
size was right, as he was quite tall, but he just glared and
thrust cash at me. It was a fifty. I almost ran out of change
taking the sale. Most peculiar."

"What did he look like?"

"Like another tourist, but slightly taller." Snodgrass'
gaze snapped to the door as a customer came in, but then he
grunted and said, "There he is, across the road. Going into
the bakery."

We turned and watched a tall, slender man, with a
dark tan, wearing jeans and a scruffy black cotton shirt look
both ways, then dart into Lovely Buns, tugging his baseball
cap low as he did so.

"You sure?" I asked.

"Yes. It was very unusual. Everyone tries on their
shoes before they buy. How would you know if they fit
otherwise? And no way was he a seven and a half."

"Anything else? Any other odd sales?"

"I don't think so. What's this all about? Should I call
Chief Swift?"

"I'm not sure what it's about yet, but I have a good
idea. No need to call Calum. It's just a thing we're working
on."

"Another one of your mysteries, eh? Maybe I should
call him."

"Nothing like that, no," I lied, not in the mood for
dealing with Calum, and knowing I had nothing to tell him
anyway beyond a feeling in my stomach.

Keeping an eye on the bakery, we filed out, sucking
in beautiful fresh air once outside on the cobbled street.

"What's going on?" asked Roger.

"He's on the case, that's what," said Forest, smiling. "But yeah, what gives? What does any of this mean?"

"I've got a feeling, that's all. This doesn't ring true about the boots, does it? Who buys them without trying them on first? Maybe if you were getting them for someone else, but it doesn't sound like he was. We need to follow him."

"I love it!" laughed Forest. "My little brother is going to solve this. You need a pipe and deerstalker."

"I might be totally wrong. Let's find out, shall we?" I had no idea what any of this meant, but I knew we had to do something. We'd promised Sheila.

The man left the bakery with an oggie in a bag, then ate it fast while dashing back down the street. He had a slight limp, and his movements were erratic, like he was close to just keeling over.

"I'll go ahead and tell you where he's going," offered Kale. "But I want a nice dinner."

"And you shall have it," I agreed. With the guys up to speed, we hung back and acted casual, letting Kale trot ahead. After a few twists and turns, Kale called for us to hurry, sounding worried. We ran after him then came to a halt in the car park.

"He's over there, in the campervan," said Kale.

"Guys, he's over there," I told them.

"Not another van," complained Forest. "Are they breeding or something?"

We watched as he climbed into the driver's seat and just sat there for a moment, fiddling with something. He turned and looked into the back, then we saw his face again. He didn't look happy.

"That's Sheila's van," I said. "The number plate's the same."

"He's nicked it?" said Roger. "Cheeky bugger. He must have done it the moment we left. Think he saw us there? You think this is what it's about? Stealing vans?"

"It can't be. And where did he get the key? We should follow him. Come on."

We slid between vans and buses, hiding our movements, then walked casually to the Land Rover and got in quickly. Safely hidden, we waited for the man to drive off, then followed.

Where was he going? Was he doing a runner, or was he up to something else? My gut told me the latter, but I'd be in a world of trouble with Calum if the thief, and possible murderer, drove away and I could have stopped him. But did we know he was the killer? No, but we knew he was a thief.

I decided we had to find out, although it meant risking this blowing up in my face. For ten minutes we drove around the outskirts of town, seemingly randomly. The campervan took several turnings down lanes only to emerge again and circle back. Then he drove to Wailing Wood before skirting the edge and driving up to the top then along the ridge until he parked up well away from the tourist areas in a remote spot.

"What's he doing?" asked Forest, craning forward.

"No idea," I said.

"Let's go find out," said Roger.

"Wait!"

But it was too late. Roger was out of the door and marching towards the campervan, looking like trouble on legs.

"He prefers to confront his issues," laughed Forest.

"This isn't a good move," I said.

"What's the other option? Keep following him? We need to do something."

"Maybe. There's no choice now anyway."

We jumped out and followed. Kale barked as he ran after Roger, warning him to be careful.

Halfway to the van, I wondered if we should have brought our hats and staves. Too late now. This one would have to play out with the magic inherent in all of us.

I just hoped it would be enough.

Showdown

"Who the hell are you?" spat the thief as he slammed the driver's door behind him and glared at us.

"We might ask you the same thing, buddy," growled Forest, flexing his muscles.

"I'm just here to enjoy the views and soak up the atmosphere," he said, looking about as much like a hiker as Forest did a big group of trees.

"You often do that in stolen vehicles, do you?" asked Roger as he stepped up beside Forest.

I groaned, as this was not the way to handle things, but it was out of my hands now. Trying not to let the situation overwhelm me, I took a deep breath, calmed myself, and opened my inner senses to see what I picked up.

As I joined the others, I got the overwhelming feeling of panic. This man was stressed, out of control, and didn't know what to do. He looked ill, like he hadn't eaten anything apart from the oggie in days. A sickly pallor signified he was bordering on malnourished. He was unstable, unpredictable, and dangerous. He was the murderer.

Kale growled at him, a deep rumble that made me sure of my first impression.

"What's your name?" I asked.

"What's yours?" he snapped, trying to keep an eye on all of us at once, but focusing on Kale.

"Bran. This is my brother, Forest, and our lodger, Roger. That's Kale."

"Seriously, you're calling me the lodger again?"

"Last one in's the lodger," crowed Forest, smirking.

"That's the rules," I agreed.

"What rules?"

"The ones we made up," I said, smiling.

"What are you talking about? Leave me alone. Go away."

"We're going nowhere. You stole this van and you killed Albert."

"Who's Albert?" he asked, frowning.

"The guy you killed. What, killed so many you can't remember? Old guy, owned the van. You left his wife a widow. We won't let you get her too," I warned, slowly moving closer along with the others, letting my power build inside.

It might not be perfect, but we could still do him some damage if we combined forces. And Kale could just bite him if it came to that.

"You're all mad. Go on, bugger off. This is my van."

"No, it's Sheila's. You stole it. I know the number plate."

"Wait here," said the gangly killer. He yanked open the door to the back of the campervan and stormed inside. We exchanged a confused look, but at least we knew he wasn't going anywhere.

"Think he's making a cuppa?" asked Roger hopefully.

"Doubt it. Probably trying to figure out how to get away without Kale chewing on his knackers."

We heard muffled moans from inside the van, then a moment later the man shoved Captain out the door. He stumbled into my arms and I caught him.

"Captain? What are you doing here?"

"Silly lanky fool made me get into the van. Tied me up and gagged me. I just got loose and then he barged in. It smells weird in there. Like wet carpet. Hello boys, how are you?" he asked, adjusting his fedora.

"You aren't dressed. What is going on?"

"Like I said, this idiot forced me into the van. Wouldn't let me get dressed. But at least I'm not cold. I always told you boys, be prepared. Now who's laughing, eh?" Captain proudly ran his hands down his long johns.

"Not us," I said.

"Did he hurt you?" asked Roger, glaring at the man.

"Like I'd let him. I can take him. He did it, you know. He killed Sheila's husband. Said he'd kill us if we didn't tell him."

"Tell him what?" asked Forest.

"Enough!" shouted the man. "What is with you? I just wanted what was mine. I followed that foul man from the campervan when he went for a walk. Idiot even left his keys in the van so I took them. Just in case. Told him I wanted the box. But he wouldn't listen. Kept pretending he didn't know what I was talking about. I knew he'd taken what was mine and switched the boxes, but he pretended he didn't understand. He shoved me and told me to get lost. Said he'd report me to the police when he got back because I was clearly up to no good. I couldn't have that."

"So you pushed him off a cliff?" I asked, shocked.

"He had it coming. I've never met anyone so rude in my life."

"You murdered him. That's pretty rude."

"I was still more polite than he was. He had a real bad attitude."

Roger made a move on the guy, but he whipped out a gun and pointed it at him. "Don't think so. I'm not an amateur. This isn't my first rodeo."

"You ride wild horses? Is that what they do at rodeos?"

"What? No," he snapped. "I mean, I've done this before."

"Shoved someone off a cliff?" I asked. "Got boxes confused? Because you've got me confused. What's this really about?

"Of course I've never pushed someone off a cliff! Although, there was that thing at a high-rise car park, but that was different. Are you all mad? Can't you see the gun? Just shut up!" He clutched his head with his free hand, clearly sick.

"Shoot him," said Captain.

"What?" I gasped, turning to him. "I haven't got a gun."

"Forest, Roger, you shoot him then."

"We haven't got guns, Captain. We aren't allowed."

"What do you mean, you aren't allowed? You're wizards."

"Yeah, and all we get are sticks and rubbish hats," I muttered.

"They are not sticks. They're staves. And don't you dare call them staffs. A wizard's staff singular, staves plural."

"Not that again!" I grumbled. "We don't need a lecture on how you like to spell things, and yes, we know it's tradition."

"Watch your attitude," warned Captain. "And you know they contain power. And those hats are precious. Don't you dare give them away."

"Whose giving their hat away?" I asked. "I never said that."

"Good."

"Are you guys soft in the head? You do know that I have a gun, right? You can see me pointing it at you?"

"Oh, don't be a daft," Captain told him. "Just hand it over and we'll call this a win for the Fairfields," he cackled, enjoying himself way more than the rest of us.

"You are, you're all lobotomised. Everyone get in." He indicated the campervan with a wave of the gun.

"I'm not going in there again," said Captain. "It's tiny. No, I think it's best you just hand over the gun and we'll be on our way."

"You'll just forget about this, will you?"

"What's your name?" I asked. "If we're going to talk, and maybe give you what you want, we need a name."

"Call me Sam," he sneered.

"Sam, game's up," crowed Captain. "Time to admit defeat."

"He needs a doctor. Why's he wearing long johns?" asked Sam.

"You wouldn't let me get dressed," said Captain.

"Everyone in." Sam indicated the van again.

"It stinks in there, I told you," yelled Captain.

"Tough. You'll do as I say."

"Won't." Captain crossed his arms and frowned like a petulant child. "I still reckon the best thing is for you to give up and we'll be on our way."

"And like I said, you'll forget about this then, will you?"

"Of course not!" said Captain. "Now I know it's you who's soft in the head. We'll take you to Chief Swift and he'll lock you up. You did commit murder, and what was this all about anyway? Drugs is it? It's always drugs."

"I do not do drugs. Or sell drugs. You don't know me. Right, if you won't get in, I'll have to make you." Sam grabbed Forest and put him in a choke hold. Forest gasped and Roger and I stepped forward but he said, "You get in the van or I blow his brains out. Don't want to get you sticky with blood and brains, do we? That'll ruin your day. Although this town and you nutters have already ruined mine. This was meant to be so easy." A sly smile crossed his face and he called out, "You in the van. Come out right now or I'll kill this man. Just to the door," he warned.

We turned as we heard the shuffling inside the van.

"There are more in there? What happened? Why didn't you tell us?" I asked.

"You didn't ask."

Helen and Sheila appeared at the door, hands tied behind their backs.

"What did he do to you?" I asked, taking in the state of them. "You look awful."

"Gee, thanks." Helen smiled weakly, clearly utterly stressed and scared.

"That man's a bully," accused Sheila. "He has a gun."

"Yes, we know," I said.

"Oh, yes, I see it. He made us get in the van. Said it must have been us. I tried to explain but he wouldn't listen. Said if we didn't tell him where it was he'd kill us."

"I don't get it," said Roger, calm as a cucumber. "How does Sam have you all?"

"He came to the house, of course," said Captain. "Helen was there to check on Sheila, and I think she wanted to see you too, Bran." Captain winked at me. "He rushed in, took us hostage, and here we are."

I turned to Sam and asked, "You mean you don't know?"

"Know what?"

"He's dafter than that duck."

"What duck?" I asked, unable to help myself.

"The daft one, of course," snapped Captain, hitching up his long johns and leaning heavily on his staff. "What's his name?"

"You mean Daffy Duck?" I asked.

"That's the one," he beamed. "Daft as Daffy Duck." Captain chuckled at his own 'joke.'

"I still have the gun," Sam reminded us. "You are all crazy. What don't I know?" he shouted.

"There's another van, you idiot," cackled Captain.

"Another van?"

"How do you know?" I asked, astonished.

"Stands to reason. It's obvious," gloated Captain. He loves to be right more than anything. The annoying thing is, he sometimes does get it right.

"Not to me," said Helen.

"You put whatever you're after in another van," said Captain. "The driver looks like Sheila's husband. The man you killed. You searched this van, assumed he had it, or Sheila did, and all along you've just got the wrong van."

"Almost right," I said.

"The man's good," said Roger.

"Guys, I'm choking here. Can we get this finished please? Anyone got an awesome idea?"

We muttered that we didn't, and all the while I was focused on Helen. Was she okay? What about Sheila? And she'd come to visit? That was a good sign. I couldn't help smiling.

"So I'm right," gloated Captain.

"That's not possible," said Sam. "This one even has the sticker. And the same curtains."

"Lots of people have the sticker. And the curtains are really common for Volkswagens," I said.

"Told you," beamed Captain. "Daft as that duck."

"You're lying! I went to the campsite and there was only one van, in the same place it was before. Don't try to trick me," he warned.

"Nobody's trying to trick you," I said. "The campsite only has a few electrical hook-ups. They're new. People with the same van left early on Friday, then Sheila and her husband took their place."

"Lots of people with campervans just pay for a night, then go park up wherever. Gives them chance to empty their toilets into the septic tanks, charge up their batteries then they can save money. There are loads of them in the woods," blurted Roger. "We met the guy who had the spot before Sheila. Oops." Roger put a hand to his mouth as we glared at him.

"Boy got dropped on his head as a child," mumbled Captain, shaking his head.

"What woods? What other people?" asked Sam, grinning madly.

"Don't know," mumbled Roger. "Just a guess."

"Take me there, right now." He pushed the gun into the side of Forest's head until he winced with the pain.

"Fine, but you have to promise to let everyone go once we get there," I said.

"I make the rules. You can go when I say you can. When I get what's mine."

"At least let Captain and the women go. He's not dressed for it and they're terrified."

"I'm dressed just fine!" growled Captain. "I'm not leaving you kids out here with this Daffy Duck. You need me."

We really didn't.

"I'm doing okay too," said Sheila. "I'm taking you down," she hissed, glaring at Sam.

"And I'm not going anywhere either," said Helen. "We're in this together." She smiled at me and my heart leapt.

But this was beyond ridiculous. This was dangerous, and someone was going to get killed. Someone was certainly going to get squashed if we tried to squeeze into the back of such a small campervan. It was meant for two, not a large family.

"Nobody leaves. Everyone in the back. Forest and Bran, you sit up front. Bran, you drive. If anyone tries anything, and I mean anything, Forest gets it. Understand?"

"Remember about the duck?" I asked Forest. "What we always used to do?" He nodded. Without hesitation, I screamed, "Duck," then snatched Captain's staff. As Sam moved the gun from Forest's head and turned it towards me, I whacked the hefty length of dense wood into the side of his head as hard as possible.

Sam dropped like a rock; the gun fell from his hand. I dashed over and picked it up, the weight strange and frightening. Knowing this simple piece of metal was just as dangerous as any wand or staff, and hating the feel of it, I told Roger, "Get the rope from the Land Rover. Tie him up good. We need to get him to Calum, and fast."

Roger nodded then ran off.

"Give me my bloody staff," ordered Captain as he wobbled, his legs giving way.

I handed it back and helped to steady him while he scowled and muttered, then turned to the others and asked, "Everyone okay?"

Amazingly, they were. A few bruised egos and a lot of confusion, but everyone was fine.

"You should have shot him," complained Captain. "Or at least blasted him."

"Our gear's in the car."

"You youngsters have so much to learn," he said. "A wizard always has his staff to hand. And his hat."

"Where's yours?" asked Forest smugly.

"On my head, you dimwit," hissed Captain.

"But it isn't pointy," said Forest.

"I'm not wearing a pointy hat. They look stupid. You think I'm going to wander around looking like a clown?" Captain tugged at his long johns then wandered over to the Land Rover and tapped his foot. "Hurry up," he called. "I'm missing lunch."

"Yeah, wouldn't want to look stupid," I muttered, then did as I was told.

Unhappy Chief

Calum did not look happy when he pulled up at the police station. We were waiting outside for him to arrive after calling him at home from a phone box. It's always strange seeing him out of his uniform, as though he's someone else. He still had that air of authority about him, but it was different, almost like he was a normal human being.

"What's this about?" he asked, eyeing us all with a weary, beaten-down droop of his shoulders. "This is my day off and I get a garbled call from you telling me you've caught a murderer. What happened?"

"This happened," said Forest as he threw open the rear door of the Land Rover then dragged Sam out by his legs and let him crash to the ground.

"You've got a man tied up and he looks dead. Did you kill him?"

"No, of course we didn't," snapped Captain. "Although these idiots should have shot him."

"What, all of us?" I asked.

"Don't get clever," he warned. "It doesn't suit you."

"He's just unconscious," I told Calum. "I whacked him over the head because he had a gun pointed at Forest. He admitted to killing Albert. We're witnesses."

"Just tell me what transpired," sighed Calum, running his hands over his head and studying us all in turn. "Sheila, Helen, are you both alright? You look shaken up."

"You would too if you were held hostage at gunpoint," snapped Helen, clearly not impressed by Calum's attitude. "You should be thanking us, not looking like this is too much work for you to bother with. Sorry to disturb you on a Sunday. We should have asked this murderer to wait until Monday to scare the life out of us. This was your job. You were meant to be tracking down this man. But oh no, you had to let your pride and your bitterness get in the way of your police work."

"Wait just one minute," snapped Calum. "Don't you dare insinuate I don't take my job seriously."

"Work and family are separate, you should know that," said Helen. "I heard all about what happened. Captain explained everything that Bran hasn't, or that I haven't been told by the insane amount of gossips in this mad town. Everyone knows you're grieving and blame Bran, but you didn't do your job. We did it. Bran and his brother and cousin did. They found your killer for you. Think you can manage to lock him up, or should we do that too? He threatened to kill us, Chief," she said it like it was a dirty word and I saw the flash of shame on Calum's face, "and where were you? Not out hunting for him, I know that much. You didn't investigate this properly, and I think that's because as soon as you knew Bran was involved, you backed off. Shame on you."

Nobody spoke as Helen glowered at Calum, her opinion of him made abundantly clear. We knew she was telling the truth in part, but her words had been harsh and exaggerated because of the stress and the adrenaline.

"It's okay," I told her. "Calum did his best."

"No, he didn't. Like you explained on the ride over here, it was you who followed the clues, you three who followed up on the shoe thing, then figured it out and found Sam. You did the work that Calum should have."

"It didn't quite happen like that, Helen, but I'm so sorry any of this happened at all," I said. "You too, Sheila. I'm so sorry you had to go through this."

"You boys found Albert's killer. That's all I care about. I can't thank you enough."

Helen glared at Calum, as if to say, "See, I told you so."

Calum was red-faced and looking about as embarrassed as I'd ever seen him. "You might be right," he conceded. "I've let my feelings for Bran get in the way of the investigation and I didn't follow through like I should have. I did what was needed, but my heart wasn't in it. Hasn't been for a long time. I'm just going through the motions. It's as though my whole world is a dream. I miss her so much." Calum broke down and he just bawled. He wasn't ashamed of the deep, almost unbearable sadness he felt, so cried freely for his loss. I think it was the release he finally needed.

Once he recovered, he was all business.

We got inside the small station, he called the rest of his team in, got the doctor out, and we went through the story, explaining what had happened and how we'd come to the conclusions we did. He didn't get angry, didn't chastise us for our actions, just listened, made notes, and was kind and patient.

Proper statements would be needed from us, but Calum said that could wait. For now, he wanted everyone to go home. The others protested, but he insisted that we needed to leave and he would finish what we'd started.

It wasn't going to happen.

With a wry smile and a theatrical sigh, he said, "Fine, you can all come. But only as far as the woods. You wait while I go and find this damn shoe box and the other campervan and then that's it. No more meddling, no more questions. And no more insults." He looked at Helen.

"I'm sorry. I didn't mean what I said," she mumbled, embarrassed. "I got carried away and it isn't my place to discuss such personal matters."

"No, it's fine," he admitted, which was beyond difficult for such a proud man. "You were right. I let personal feelings get in the way. I owe everyone an apology. But most of all I owe Sheila an apology. I'm sorry."

"I forgive you," she said.

With that, it was like a weight was lifted off his shoulders. Calum visibly relaxed, the years of stress lightened to a burden more bearable.

For a moment, as he nodded to Sheila then glanced my way, I thought maybe he was going to say he forgave me. His mouth opened, but then he closed it again. The words never came. Maybe one day. But not today.

We waited in the Land Rover while Calum went to find the young dude with the mystery shoe box. It took a while, and none of us said much while we sat there. Apart from Captain, who grumbled the whole time about his day being out of whack and needing an extra episode of The X-Files to make up for it.

When Calum finally returned, it was with the shoe box in a sealed plastic bag. We clamoured around, keen for closure. What had this all been about?

"Come on, man, what's the mystery? What's in the box?" asked Captain, trying to prod the evidence with his staff.

Calum took a step back and wagged a finger at Captain. "Just like you said. Size seven and a half walking boots." He shrugged.

"No, it can't be," I said. "This can't just be over him hiding a pair of boots. Nobody kills over boots. Do they?"

Calum smiled at me, his eyes alight with mirth. Something had changed in him. He was almost like the man I remembered from years before. "Ha, gotcha!" he laughed, then was suddenly serious. "Sorry, Sheila, I didn't mean to make light of what is a very traumatic time."

"That's okay. But come on, tell us. It isn't just boots, is it?"

"No. There are rolls of notes in the boots. Rammed in then covered with paper. All in fifties, by the looks of it.

It's a lot of money. For whatever reason, Sam, and I doubt that's his real name, stuffed money in the boots then hid them in the campervan. We'll find out why, but he was clearly worried someone would take it from him, so stashed it out of the way to retrieve later. When he went to get it back, he just found regular boots in Sheila's van so confronted Albert and we all know what happened next."

Everyone chatted excitedly about what the reason could possibly be, even Sheila, but it was obvious she needed some looking after. The poor woman was beyond drained. I told the others to get seated and that we'd go home, then wandered over to Calum as he stowed the evidence in the police car.

"She didn't mean that," I said kindly. "Helen was just stressed."

"She was right," he mumbled, still hunched over his car, not looking at me. "I just can't put this behind me, Bran. I can't forgive you. How could you do it to my little girl? To your wife?"

"I know this isn't the time, or the place, but here goes. I spoke to the guys about what you said. About the car. Roger knows cars, and he insists there is no way mine could have been like that. It had its MOT, it had been serviced. Brakes don't wear that way, Calum, neither do brake lines. He assured me it was the result of the crash, or you read more into it than you should have because you were grieving. I loved her, Calum. I'd never put her in danger. You know that. You have to believe me."

"I wish I could, but I know what I saw. I may not be an expert when it comes to cars, but I believe my own eyes."

"But the insurance inspector didn't say any of this. They agreed it was an accident, and that the car was sound. You have to accept that."

"Maybe I will. I'm sorry, Bran, I know I've treated you badly, but my baby, my daughter, the light of my life, is dead. The car was a wreck. You were negligent. I don't think you set out to hurt her, of course I don't, but it isn't right.

Maybe we can be more civil from now on, and that's on me and I apologise, but I'm not ready to forgive. Not yet."

He turned to me and our eyes met. We nodded to each other and then he went over to the others to arrange taking statements the following day. It would be a whirlwind of police activity, interviews, a large investigation, and a lot of chastising for how we'd gone about this, but Calum assured us we wouldn't be in any trouble beyond a rap on the knuckles for being rather foolhardy.

And then he left. And we went home.

Tuesday Morning

"Standin', that doesn't go there. How many times do I have to tell you? Come on, you know better than that."

"Standin' Yergarden released a torrent of quick-fire excuses followed by what I've come to recognise as gnomish swear words I still, thankfully, don't understand. He did, however, reluctantly remove the joss stick from a rather inappropriate place on a wooden statue of a fertility charm.

The other gnomes laughed and pointed at him, enjoying nothing more than when one of them got told off.

I chuckled, pleased life was finally back to as normal as it ever gets in Little Hope.

Kale shot up into a sitting position from his bed, ears primed, nose twitching, tail sweeping back and forth across the floor.

My palms grew sweaty and my heart hammered in my chest as I waited with bated breath. Maybe this would be her. All morning I'd been a bag of nerves, wondering if Helen would come to visit or if I'd blown it entirely with the way I'd acted and the conversations she'd overheard with Calum.

It wasn't her. A customer came through the door cautiously, peered around, then seemingly decided Bran's Dream wasn't for him. He left without even making eye contact. Kale and I sighed; it about summed up our mood.

After the madness of the Sunday, then the questions we'd all faced on Monday, Helen and I hadn't had much time to talk, and she was rather aloof and uncommunicative. I'd taken a step back when really I wanted to take two forward, but it seemed clear this had been too much for her and I guess I wasn't the person she'd thought I was. Did she see me as a broken man who couldn't put the loss of his wife behind him? She'd obviously been given all the gossip, so knew my story and the struggles I'd faced. Now she knew the whole sorry situation with Calum. Would she think I was the kind of man who would risk other people's lives like that?

Did she blame me for the way I'd got her and everyone else involved in uncovering the murderer? Everyone's lives had been put at risk. I knew I wasn't at fault for that. None of us knew Sam would act that way, and it had happened so fast, but the fact it had happened at all was still a lot for anyone to handle. Being thrust into our chaotic, magic-infused world would terrify most people, and when you added in my family, then I'd understand completely if she backed away from what I had to accept wasn't even the beginnings of a relationship yet.

Even the news Calum gave us about why Sam—it turns out it was his real name—had stashed the money didn't offer any satisfaction. Sam refused to divulge where he'd got the cash from, and point-blank admitted that he'd rather go to prison for what he insisted was killing Albert by accident, than tell why he hid it. Calum's professional opinion was that someone was obviously after Sam for the money and had tracked him down so he'd hidden it just in case they caught up with him. When he thought the coast was clear, he'd gone to retrieve it, then the ensuing madness happened.

Sam would be tried for murder, but was sticking to his story and insisting it was an accident, although that certainly didn't mean he wasn't in a world of trouble for kidnap, owning an illegal weapon, and numerous other acts. What the outcome would be nobody knew, but he'd be locked up for a long time, that was for certain.

Sheila's daughter came and picked her up from the cloying prison that was Captain's lair, where she'd stayed until she was told she could go home. The campervan was sold to Landrie at the campsite, who said it would make an excellent feature as it was tied to a murder. Sheila was just glad to be rid of it, insisting her touring days were over.

I felt happy we'd found closure, at least of a sort, for Sheila, but like I'd lost more than I'd gained. Helen was so great, and I knew I'd made a mess of it. The guys probably wouldn't get the renovation job, we'd never get to know each other, and it wouldn't surprise me if she moved away, certain the whole thing had been a terrible mistake and our town, and me and my family, were not worth the hassle we most clearly were.

The fact we still didn't know the reason why Sam was hiding money bugged me no end, same as everyone else. Forest and Roger, even Dad and Uncle Frank, had been calling repeatedly just to see if I'd heard anything new. How would I? It wasn't like Calum was going to ring me up and tell me about every update to the case. We were done with it now, and it would most likely drag on for months before Sam was sentenced, and even then it looked like we'd never get all the facts.

The phone rang yet again, so I answered it with a weary, "Look, I'll let you know if I hear anything more, okay?"

"Bran?"

"Um, Calum, is that you?"

"Yes. Turn on the news," he said gruffly, then hung up.

Intrigued, and amazed Calum had called for any reason, I turned on the small TV in the cubby. The local news was running on BBC1.

"...Sam 'The Bank' Taylor. Having been in hiding for almost fifteen years, it appears he's finally been captured, thanks to some local amateur sleuths."

I groaned as the news continued. The gossip grapevine was clearly still functioning as well as ever.

"Wanted in conjunction with his part in a series of armed robberies starting almost two decades ago, those caught always swore they knew nothing of either him or his whereabouts. Is it a coincidence," the young news reporter asked, "that within days of the men convicted of the holdups being released, Sam is finally captured, seemingly on the run from those he once worked with? With his involvement in the mysterious death of a tourist now confirmed, we will let you know more about 'The Bank' as the story unfolds."

I turned off the TV. None of this would bring Albert back to life.

The bell jangled wildly for the hundredth time, grating on my nerves.

With a sigh, I looked up, knowing my hopes would be dashed once more.

Kale yelped, tail wagging.

Helen stormed through the door, and I vowed I'd rip the stupid bell down this very day. She marched through the shop, face grim and determined, eyes locked on me.

"Do not," she warned, "say a word."

"I—"

Helen leaned over the counter, put a finger on my lips to quiet me, then slowly removed it. "Not a word."

She smiled. And kissed me.

I decided to keep the bell.

I send out emails when new books are published, so please sign up for news about releases and sales. No spam. Just book updates. Promise.

Ready for the next in the series? Wizardly Eyes sees Bran, Kale, and the gang in even more bother, and Grenadine wants in on the action. After all, eight eyes are better than two, right?

From the Author

As an indie writer, exposure is very important. If you enjoyed this wizard cozy mystery then you can help. It's as simple as leaving a review. The more reviews, the more the book will be seen. This helps to support me by encouraging sales.

Writing is my full-time job, so please consider a review or a rating.

How did you find Bran and the others? I hope I've managed to combine family life with the paranormal, and enough mystery to keep you entertained. Be sure to check out the next in the series. Now we've introduced many of the main characters, we can begin to delve deeper into their lives and follow along with their magical ways.

Thanks for reading.

Tyler

Feel free to email me any time at contact@authortylerrhodes.com or visit my website at www.authortylerrhodes.com. And be sure to stay updated about new releases. You'll hear about them first. No spam, just book updates.

You can also follow me on Amazon.

Connect with me on Facebook.

Printed in Great Britain
by Amazon